The Echoing Room A Psychological Thriller

Kraken

Published by Kraken, 2024.

This is a work of fiction. Similarities to real people, places, or events are entirely coincidental.

THE ECHOING ROOM A PSYCHOLOGICAL THRILLER

First edition. October 7, 2024.

Copyright © 2024 Kraken.

ISBN: 979-8227716781

Written by Kraken.

Table of Contents

Chapter 1: The Cry of Midnight 1
Chapter 2: The First Session 3
Chapter 3: Shadows of the Past 6
Chapter 5: Reflections in the Dark 11
Chapter 6: Shadows of Whispering Pines 13
Chapter 7: The Circle of Shadows 16
Chapter 8: Unspoken Truths 19
Chapter 9: The Weight of Secrets 22
Chapter 10: The Unraveling Net 25
Chapter 11: In the Shadows 28
Chapter 12: The Hidden Layers 31
Chapter 13: The Edge of Revelation 34
Chapter 14: The Unexpected Ally 37
Chapter 15: The Deepest Shadows 40
Chapter 16: The Web Tightens 43
Chapter 17: The Price of Truth 45
Chapter 18: The Unraveling Truth 48
Chapter 19: The Hidden Camera 50
Chapter 20: The Final Confrontation 53
Chapter 21: The Unraveling Truth 56
Chapter 22: Shadows in the Past 58
Chapter 23: The Final Ceremony 61
Chapter 24: Unraveling the Web 64
Chapter 25: The Mask Uncovered 66
Chapter 26: The Shattered Illusion 69
Chapter 27: The Final Showdown 71
Chapter 28: Aftermath and Reflection 74
Chapter 29: New Beginnings 76
Chapter 30: The Final Echo 78

Chapter 1: The Cry of Midnight

The night was oppressive, with a thick fog that pressed against the windows as if they were ghostly hands. Evelyn sat up on the bed, her body drenched in an icy sweat. The heart pounded in his chest as his fingers clutched the sheets, his knuckles whitening against the dark fabric. The echo of the scream that had escaped from his throat still reverberated in his ears, fading into the silence of the room.

The clock next to her bed flickered in the darkness: 3:33 in the morning, the same time she always marked when these nightmares assailed her. With the back of her hand, she wiped her wet forehead, trying to breathe through the fear that clung to her like a second skin. Outside, the world was still, and the fog enveloped Millbrook in a blanket of deathly silence. Only the distant purr of a passing car reminded him that, somewhere outside this bedroom, life was going on.

Evelyn forced herself to calm down. It was just another nightmare. The day had to pass, and today was important. A new patient was waiting for her. Another soul to dissect, to fix. It was the routine that kept her sane, preventing her from thinking too much about what those dreams might mean.

She swung her legs on the edge of the bed and stood up, her nightgown pressed against her wet skin. The soft creak of the wooden floor beneath his feet felt like a whisper of something more sinister. He brushed it off and went to the bathroom to pour cold water on his face.

In the mirror, she barely recognized herself. Sunken eyes, skin that is too pale, hair disheveled and stuck to the forehead. She was no stranger to exhaustion. The therapy had that effect on people, also on healers. However, now there was something different. Something that tugged at the edges of his memory, something that the nightmare had stirred up but refused to reveal.

He dressed quietly, moving through the familiar movements of his morning routine. The coffee machine came alive in the kitchen as the fog outside grew denser, swallowing the world in a dull gray haze. Evelyn was standing by the window, cup in hand, staring into nothingness. The feeling was getting stronger and stronger, a fear that gnawed at him that today was the beginning of something... different. Uncontrollable.

His phone rang on the counter. A message from his assistant. *Your appointment at 9 AM is confirmed. Lila Matthews, first session.*

Evelyn sighed, turning away from the window. She still had time before she had to leave, but the heaviness in her chest remained, like an anchor that dragged her deeper into something she didn't understand.

"The carousel never stops spinning."

The phrase came to his mind, spontaneously. It left a bitter taste in his mouth. I couldn't locate where I'd heard it before, but it felt too familiar, too close. He blinked, setting the cup down on the floor with a clatter that echoed through the empty kitchen.

Today I would meet Lila. Today, something would begin. He felt it in the marrow of his bones.

Chapter 2: The First Session

Dr. Evelyn Caldwell's office was a sanctuary of calm, carefully selected to exude warmth and professionalism. The dim lighting, muted colors, and plush furnishings created a cocoon of serenity. It was designed to make patients feel safe, to trust him with their darkest secrets. Evelyn took a deep breath, preparing for the session ahead. His gaze was fixed on the clock on the wall. It was almost 9 in the morning.

The doorbell rang, a bell that rang louder than usual in the stillness. Evelyn got up from her chair and walked to the entrance of her office, opening the door to reveal her new patient. Lila Matthews was there, a frail figure wrapped in a heavy, oversized coat. Her eyes were an eerie blue, shadowed by a deep sadness that seemed to overwhelm her.

"Miss Matthews?" Evelyn asked gently.

Lila nodded, lowering her gaze to the ground. "Yes. Please call me Lila.

Evelyn stepped aside to let Lila in, her professional attitude masking the discomfort that had settled in her stomach. When Lila entered the office, Evelyn could see the trembling in her hands, the way her shoulders seemed perpetually hunched over, as if preparing for an invisible storm.

"Please sit down," Evelyn said, pointing to the sofa. Lila sat up slowly, her movements cautious and deliberate. Evelyn sat down in front of Lila, her notebook ready.

"Thank you for coming today, Lila. How are you feeling?

Lila moved uncomfortably. "Nervous. I've never done this before."

Evelyn smiled reassuringly. "It's perfectly normal to feel that way. We will go step by step. Why don't you start by telling me what brings you here today?

Lila hesitated, and her eyes swept across the room as if searching for the right words. "I... I don't know where to start. I've been having these dreams, and... And there is a phrase that keeps coming up. 'The carousel never stops spinning.'"

The phrase hit Evelyn like a splash of cold water. He struggled to keep his composure, his heart racing with an unsettling familiarity. —What do you think this phrase means?

Lila's hands wrung in her lap. "I don't know. It feels like he's trying to tell me something. But I don't understand what."

Evelyn leaned forward slightly, her curiosity piqued. "Can you tell me more about these dreams?"

Lila's voice trembled. "They are... they are always the same. I'm on a carousel, and it's moving, but it's like... I can't get off, I'm stuck. And there are these people with masks..."

The room seemed to grow cold as Lila spoke. Evelyn's mind raced with fragments of her own memories, images of carousels and masked figures that merged with Lila's description. He put aside his growing discomfort and focused on Lila's story.

"Can you describe these people with masks?" Evelyn asked, her voice firm despite the turmoil inside.

Lila shuddered. "They wear animal masks. There is a lion, a wolf... They don't speak. Simply... Observe."

Evelyn's pulse quickened. He scribbled notes furiously, his mind reeling from parallels with his own fragmented memories. "Lila, do you remember anything else from these dreams? Is there anything that stands out?

Lila's eyes filled with tears. "There's a sound, like a music box. Play this tune that doesn't stop. And sometimes, there's this feeling... Like they're watching me, even when I wake up."

The room was silent, except for the soft ticking of the clock. Evelyn's thoughts were a swirl of fear and fascination. "Lila, thank you for sharing that with me. It's important that we explore these feelings further. I think there may be connections that we need to discover."

Lila nodded, wiping her eyes. "I hope so. I need to understand what's happening to me."

As the session came to an end, Evelyn watched Lila leave, her steps slow and hesitant. Evelyn felt the weight of the conversation sit heavily on her shoulders. She couldn't shake the feeling that Lila's case was more than just a routine therapy session. There was something deeply unsettling about the connection between Lila's nightmares and her own past.

Evelyn closed the door behind Lila and sat down again, her mind a storm of thoughts and fears. The phrase "The carousel never stops spinning" echoed in his mind, an ominous reminder that today marked the beginning of a journey into the darkest corners of his own soul.

Chapter 3: Shadows of the Past

The day after Lila's session had been a whirlwind of routine tasks and fleeting moments of distraction. As he drove home, the mist still clung to Millbrook like a ghostly veil. The familiar streets, usually a consolation, now seemed oppressive and strange.

At home, Evelyn tried to focus on her family. Her husband, Thomas, was already at the dining room table, working on paperwork for his job. Her teenage daughter, Zoe, was in her room, a sanctuary of teenage clutter and noise.

"A long day?" Thomas asked, without looking up from his papers.

Evelyn nodded, forcing a smile as she slid into the chair in front of him. "You could say that."

Thomas looked up, worry etched into his features. "You look a little pale. Everything is fine?"

Evelyn shrugged in concern. "Just a long session. It's nothing."

Thomas' eyes paused on her for a moment before returning to his work. Evelyn was grateful for the silence. He needed it to process the disturbing details of his session with Lila. The carousel, the masked figures, everything resounded with a deep and unsettling echo.

After dinner, Evelyn retired to her study, a small, cozy room filled with books and therapeutic artifacts. He sat at his desk, trying to drown out the fog that had crept into his thoughts. His mind kept spinning on the phrase "The carousel never stops spinning."

He reached for his old diary, a dusty, leather-bound book he hadn't opened in years. The familiar scent of paper and aged ink filled the air as I flipped through the pages. The entries were filled with fragmented thoughts and therapeutic insights from their early days in practice. Nothing caught the eye until it reached the last pages, where its handwriting became erratic.

"Carousel," he murmured, tracing a specific passage with his finger. It was a vague note about a recurring dream from her childhood: a carousel, masks, and an overwhelming sense of being trapped.

His heart raced as he read the entry. The details were eerily similar to Lila's description. Could it be possible that these dreams were not a mere coincidence but were connected to something more sinister? Something that had buried it so deeply that it now threatened to come to the surface?

As she pondered this, a knock on the door startled her. Zoe stood there, with an expression mixed with curiosity and concern.

"Mom, are you okay?" Zoe asked, entering the room.

Evelyn forced a smile. "I'm just working on some old notes. There's nothing to worry about."

Zoe's gaze lingered on the diary. "It looks like you've been digging up some old stuff. Is it something from your job?

"Something like that," Evelyn replied, closing the diary with a sigh. "Sometimes, it helps to revisit old memories."

Zoe shrugged. "Well, if you need anything, I'm here."

"Thank you, honey," Evelyn said, trying to sound reassuring.

When Zoe left, Evelyn felt a twinge of guilt. She had always prided herself on being emotionally available to her family, but lately, her work was consuming her. The shadows of his past seemed to be closing, blurring the line between his professional life and his personal demons.

The next day, Evelyn decided to visit her mentor, Dr. Franklin Reid, for guidance. His office was a quiet retreat filled with the smell of old books and the soft hum of classical music. He recounted Lila's case and the disturbing details that had come to light.

Dr. Reid listened intently, with an inscrutable expression. "It seems that Lila's experience has triggered something in you, Evelyn. It's not uncommon for therapists to feel a connection to their patients' traumas."

Evelyn nodded, though her uneasiness persisted. "But what if it's more than that? What if there's something I'm missing?"

Reid's eyes narrowed thoughtfully. "Sometimes, our minds try to protect us from painful memories. It's possible that Lila's case is unlocking something buried in your own past. It might be worth exploring these connections further."

Evelyn left Reid's office feeling calm and uneasy. As she walked to her car, she couldn't shake the feeling that her research into Lila's past might unearth more than she was prepared to handle. The carousel of her own memories seemed to be spinning out of control, and she got caught up in its relentless spin.

Chapter 4: Unraveling Threads

The next few days were a blur of sleepless nights and fragmented thoughts for Evelyn. His dreams, once sporadic and unsettling, had become unforgiving. Each night was haunted by the same carousel, the same masked figures, and the same oppressive feeling of being trapped.

In her waking hours, Evelyn would give herself to her work, hoping that the distraction might offer her some relief. He meticulously reviewed Lila's case notes, looking for any clues that might shed light on the mysterious phrase and its connection to his own past.

One morning, as she sat at her desk, the phone rang. It was Detective Marcus Holloway, the local investigator with whom he had spoken briefly about the recent series of murders. His voice was concise and professional.

"Dr. Caldwell, I need to ask you a few more questions about Lila Matthews," Holloway said. "Could we meet today?"

Evelyn agreed, and they agreed to meet at a coffee shop near her office. The place was bustling with the hustle and bustle of the morning, the clatter of cups and the murmur of conversations filled the air. Holloway arrived promptly, with a very simple demeanor. He was a tall, rough-faced man who spoke of long hours of work and difficult cases.

"Dr. Caldwell," Holloway said, sitting across from her, "I've been investigating the recent Millbrook murders. All the victims look like you in some way, and they all have ties to Whispering Pines."

Evelyn stiffened. —What do you mean by the links with Whispering Pines?

Holloway leaned forward. "They were all former residents of the village. We are investigating any connections they may have had. Did you mention that Lila Matthews has experience there as well?

"Yes," Evelyn said in a firm voice. "She also grew up in Whispering Pines. We've been discovering some disturbing details in his sessions, which seem to be related to my own past."

Holloway's eyes narrowed. "I need you to be honest with me, Dr. Caldwell. Do you think there's a connection between your past, Lila's, and these murders?"

Evelyn hesitated, the weight of her knowledge pressing on her. "There's something unsettling about these connections. Lila's case has brought back memories that I thought I had forgotten a long time ago. But I can't be sure how they all fit together."

Holloway nodded thoughtfully. "We are investigating any leads that may connect the victims. If you remember anything else, it could be crucial to our investigation."

When Evelyn left the cafeteria, her mind raced. The conversation with Holloway had only increased his growing sense of paranoia. The murders, Lila's case, and her own repressed memories were woven into a web of darkness that seemed to be closing in on her.

Later that day, Evelyn decided to contact her sister, Diane. They hadn't spoken in years, but Evelyn felt that Diane might hold the key to unraveling some of the mysteries surrounding her past. Diane was still living in Whispering Pines, and Evelyn hoped to be able to provide some insight into their shared history.

The phone call was awkward, full of tentative jokes and unspoken tension. Diane agreed to meet Evelyn at a restaurant halfway between their homes. When Evelyn arrived, she found Diane already seated, her expression a mixture of curiosity and caution.

"Evelyn," Diane said, her voice soft but cautious. "It's been a long time."

"Yes, he has," Evelyn replied, sitting down. "I'm sorry to meddle in this way, but I need your help."

Diane narrowed her eyes. "Help with what?"

Evelyn took a deep breath. "I'm dealing with some... Haunting memories of our childhood. I think they might be connected to what's happening now. I need to understand more about Mom and what happened back then."

Diane's face darkened. "You're bringing old wounds to light. Why now?"

"I've been working with a patient who has similar experiences," Evelyn said. "And it's triggered something in me. I need to know the truth."

Diane sighed, her gaze drifting to the window. "Mom was involved with Gabriel Stone. He was... influential in Whispering Pines. I always suspected there was something dark about him, but I never knew the full extent."

The name of Gabriel Stone made Evelyn shudder. He had heard it before, briefly in his own fragmented memories and now from Diane's lips.

"Do you know where I can find it?" Evelyn asked, her voice barely above a whisper.

Diane looked at her with a mixture of fear and resignation. "He runs a wellness retreat on the outskirts of the city. It is said that it is a place to heal, but I have always had my doubts."

Evelyn felt a chill. The name of Gabriel Stone and retirement were now firmly etched in his mind. The pieces of the puzzle were beginning to fall into place, but the whole picture was still shrouded in darkness.

As she left the restaurant, Evelyn's resolve hardened. He needed to face the past, no matter how dangerous it might be. The echoes of her childhood were calling her back to Whispering Pines, and she was determined to face them head-on.

Chapter 5: Reflections in the Dark

The day was cloudy as Evelyn drove through the misty streets of Millbrook, her thoughts consumed by the revelation about Gabriel Stone. The name resonated with an unsettling familiarity, and his desire to confront the truth about his past grew stronger.

Upon arriving at his office, he found it difficult to focus on his clients. The sessions felt mechanical, his mind frequently returning to the conversation with Diane. He couldn't shake the feeling that the answers he was looking for were beyond the confines of his safe, familiar city.

That night, while Evelyn sat at her desk, she played the recordings of her sessions with Lila, looking for any overlooked details that might link her own past to the sinister group Diane had mentioned. The tapes were filled with fragmented memories of Lila and Evelyn's attempts to guide her through the trauma, but one session in particular stood out.

Lila's voice, tense and tearful, spoke of a recurring dream involving a carousel, masked figures, and a feeling of suffocation. Evelyn's heart raced as she listened to the description. The dream was eerily similar to his own fragmented memories and the diary entries he had reviewed.

A knock on the office door brought her out of her thoughts. It was Thomas, his face wrinkled with worry. "Evelyn, we need to talk."

She nodded, her heart sinking. "Sure, what's on your mind?"

Thomas entered, taking a seat across from her. "I've noticed that you've been distant lately. This case has really taken its toll on you, hasn't it?

Evelyn forced a smile. "It's been a lot to handle. But I'm getting by."

Thomas shook his head. "That's not what worries me. You're not sleeping well and you've been distracted. I know you're doing your job, but you have to take care of yourself."

Evelyn's eyes filled with frustration. "I'm fine, Thomas. I just need to see this to the end."

Thomas's expression softened. "I just want you to be okay. You've always been the strong one, but you don't have to carry this burden alone."

His words dragged on as he walked out of his office. Evelyn felt a twinge of guilt, knowing that her personal struggles were affecting her family. I wanted to reassure him, but the weight of his own fears and doubts was overwhelming.

Later that night, Evelyn lay in bed, her mind racing. I couldn't ignore the feeling that Gabriel Stone was a key figure in the dark history I was trying to uncover. His thoughts went back to the old photograph he'd found among his mother's belongings years ago: an image of a group of people wearing masks and gathered around a carousel. It was a disturbing image that had been buried in the recesses of his memory.

Unable to sleep, Evelyn decided to revisit her mother's old belongings, stored in a dusty attic. The dim attic light cast long shadows as he rummaged through boxes of old photographs, letters, and memorabilia. Finally, he found the photograph he had remembered. The faces were blurred and obscured by the masks, but the carousel was unmistakable.

As Evelyn examined the photograph, she noticed something she had overlooked before: a small symbol engraved on the base of the carousel. It was a carousel horse with a distinctive design. His heart was pounding as he realized that it resembled the symbol Diane had mentioned, which was worn by many of the city's prominent figures.

The photograph left her with more questions than answers. What had his mother been involved in? How did Gabriel Stone and The Circle fit into the bigger picture? The connections were growing more and more unsettling, and Evelyn's determination to uncover the truth grew stronger.

The next day, Evelyn decided to take a more proactive approach. She planned a visit to Whispering Pines, intending to learn more about Gabriel Stone and his wellness retreat. As she prepared for the trip, she felt a mixture of anxiety and determination. The journey to his past was fraught with danger, but it was a path he needed to follow.

As Evelyn made her way toward Whispering Pines, the fog seemed to thicken, reflecting the murky depths of her investigation. The city rose in the distance, shrouded in mist and mystery. He knew that what awaited him there would be both revealing and dangerous.

Chapter 6: Shadows of Whispering Pines

The trip to Whispering Pines was a winding journey through fog-clogged roads and dense forest. Evelyn's hands gripped the steering wheel tightly, her knuckles white with tension. The familiar landscape, though shrouded in fog, awakened deep-seated memories and fears. As he neared the outskirts of the city, his heart raced with anticipation and dread.

The town of Whispering Pines emerged from the fog, its picturesque appearance belied the darkness Evelyn knew lurked beneath its surface. The streets were eerily quiet, occasionally a car passing by as if driven by ghosts. Evelyn parked the car near the old restaurant where she had met Diane and got out, the cool, humid air filling her lungs.

Inside the restaurant, the atmosphere contrasted with the fog outside. The neon lights and the smell of freshly brewed coffee were comforting, but Evelyn's mind was far from calm. He sat in a booth near the window, scanning the room for any sign of Diane.

After a short wait, Diane arrived, with a cautious demeanor. He slid into the cockpit in front of Evelyn, his expression a mixture of reluctance and determination. "What brings you back here, Evelyn?" Diane asked quietly.

"I need to know more about Gabriel Stone and his retirement," Evelyn said, leaning forward. – You mentioned that he runs a wellness retreat on the outskirts of the city. I need to know more about it."

Diane looked around the restaurant, her eyes wary. "Gabriel Stone has always been a shadowy figure. His retirement is known for its secrecy, but there are rumors. People say he's still involved with the old group, The Circle.

Evelyn's pulse quickened. "What kind of rumors?"

"Whispered stories about strange rituals, people disappearing, and a sense of fear that hangs over retirement," Diane explained. "The people distrust him, but no one dares to speak openly."

Evelyn frowned, processing the information. "Do you know how I can get in touch with him or visit the retreat?"

Diane hesitated, then handed Evelyn a small piece of paper. "This is the direction of withdrawal. It's insulated and you'll have to be careful. People don't like outsiders snooping around."

Evelyn took the paper and nodded, gratitude mixed with apprehension. "Thank you, Diane." I'll be cautious."

When Diane left, Evelyn finished her coffee and prepared to drive to the retreat. The fog outside seemed to thicken as I walked out of the restaurant, and the path to the retreat became more and more isolated. The trees stood like silent sentinels, their gnarled branches stretching out as if to catch her.

After what seemed like hours, Evelyn finally arrived at the entrance of the retreat. The door was made of wrought iron, adorned with intricate designs that seemed almost ornamental, yet imposing. One sign read, "Gabriel Stone's Retirement: Road to Renewal."

Evelyn hesitated before pushing open the door. The shelter was a sprawling enclosure nestled deep in the forest. The buildings were modern but designed to blend in with the natural surroundings. It was an unsettling juxtaposition of serene architecture and foreboding atmosphere.

As she walked down the gravel road, she was greeted by a reception area that felt more like a fortress than a welcoming space. The receptionist, a stern woman with piercing eyes, looked at Evelyn with thinly veiled suspicion.

"I'm here to see Gabriel Stone," Evelyn said, her voice firm despite the tension in her chest.

The receptionist's expression remained neutral. "Mr. Stone is not available for unscheduled visits. Do you have a date?"

Evelyn shook her head. "No, but it's important. Please let him know I'm here."

The receptionist's gaze hardened. "I'm afraid I can't let you go without an appointment. You should go."

Evelyn's frustration grew, but she forced herself to stay calm. "Please, this is urgent. I need to talk to him about some sensitive matters."

The receptionist's expression softened slightly. "Wait here."

Moments later, a man in a fancy suit appeared. He had an air of authority and a charming smile that made Evelyn's skin crawl. "I'm Daniel, Mr. Stone's assistant. What is it about?

Evelyn took a deep breath. "I need to talk to Mr. Stone about some past connections and recent events. It's crucial."

Daniel's smile wavered slightly. "Mr. Stone has a very busy schedule. I'll see if he's available for a short meeting."

As Daniel walked away, Evelyn felt a knot of anxiety tighten in her stomach. He glanced around the reception area, noticing the opulent décor and the sense of controlled calm. It felt like a façade, hiding something much darker.

After a tense wait, Daniel returned. "Mr. Stone will see you." Follow me."

Evelyn followed him through a series of winding corridors until they reached an imposing office door. Daniel knocked on the door and then opened it, revealing a spacious office with large windows overlooking the retreat grounds. Gabriel Stone was sitting behind a large desk, with a calm and collected demeanor.

"Dr. Caldwell," Stone said, rising to greet her with a warm but chilling smile. "What a pleasure to meet you. How can I help you today?"

Evelyn forced herself to look him in the eye. "Mr. Stone, I have some questions about retirement and its history. I think there may be connections to my past that need to be addressed."

Stone's smile never wavered, but his eyes narrowed slightly. "I'm sure we can discuss everything you need to know. Please sit down."

When Evelyn sat down, she felt a growing sense of unease. The answers he sought were within his grasp, but the path to them was fraught with danger. He steeled himself for the conversation ahead, knowing that uncovering the truth would require more than courage—it would require facing the shadows of his own past.

Chapter 7: The Circle of Shadows

Evelyn sat across from Gabriel Stone, trying to keep her composure under the weight of his intense gaze. The office, with its serene décor and expansive windows, looked like an elaborate setting to mask the darkness Evelyn suspected lay beneath. Stone's gentle demeanor only increased his uneasiness.

"Dr. Caldwell, I understand that you are concerned about our retirement," Stone began, in a calm, measured voice. "Please share with me what you're worried about."

Evelyn took a deep breath. "I've been researching some disturbing connections between this retirement and my past. I have learned about a group called The Circle and its possible involvement in my childhood trauma. I need to know if there is any connection between The Circle and this retreat."

Stone's expression remained neutral, but Evelyn noticed a gleam of something in her eyes, a faint hint of recognition or perhaps apprehension. "The Circle? That's a name I haven't heard in many years. What makes you believe there's a connection here?

Evelyn didn't want to reveal too soon. "I have found information that suggests that some of the people associated with The Circle might have been involved in the realization of this retreat. I'm trying to piece together what really happened and how it relates to my own experiences."

Stone leaned back in his chair, studying it with a contemplative expression. "Our retreat is dedicated to healing and personal growth. We focus on helping people overcome their past traumas. If there has been any misunderstanding or miscommunication, I assure you that it will be fixed."

Evelyn sensed that Stone was being evasive. "I need to know more about the history of retirement. What were its origins? Was there any member of El Círculo involved in its establishment?

Stone's eyes narrowed slightly. "The retreat has been under various directions over the years. Our current focus is on moving forward, not dwelling on the past. I suggest focusing on the present and the benefits we offer our customers."

Evelyn felt a surge of frustration, but she kept her composure. "I need to talk to someone who was here during the early years of retirement. It's crucial to understanding the bigger picture."

Stone's smile didn't reach his eyes. "That could be difficult. Many of our early records are confidential and access to them requires special authorization. I can't promise you that you will find the answers you are looking for, but I will consider your request."

Before Evelyn could answer, Daniel reappeared at the door. "Mr. Stone, there's someone here who insists on talking to you."

Stone's smile returned, though it was colder now. "Please excuse me for a moment. I'll be right back."

As Stone left the office, Evelyn took the opportunity to examine her surroundings more closely. The room was meticulously organized, with shelves filled with self-help and personal development books. His gaze fell on a framed photograph on the desk: a group of people in ceremonial masks gathered around a carousel. The image made his blood run cold.

The door opened and Stone returned, now accompanied by a stern-looking man in a dark suit. "This is Richard, our head of security. "He'll help you with any further investigations," Stone said, his tone polite but firm.

Richard's expression was inscrutable as he reached out. "Dr. Caldwell, I understand you have some questions about the history of the retreat. I'll be your point of contact from now on."

Evelyn shook his hand, trying to gauge his intentions. "Thank you, Richard. I hope to gain some clarity about the past and its connections to retirement."

Richard nodded, his gaze fixed. "I will arrange a time for you to review the relevant records. In the meantime, remember that the retreat is focused on positive change and healing."

As Evelyn left the office, she felt a growing sense of urgency. The photograph had confirmed his fears: the Circle's influence was probably deeper than he had imagined. The next step was to dig deeper into the history of the retreat and find out what Stone and his associates were hiding.

Back in her car, Evelyn noticed a strange figure lurking near the driveway, a man who quickly disappeared as she approached. His uneasiness deepened as he moved away from the retreat, the fog looking thicker and more oppressive than before.

As he returned to Millbrook, his mind was filled with questions and concerns. What secrets are hidden behind the façade of Gabriel Stone's retreat? And how far would he have to go to discover the truth about The Circle and his own past?

Chapter 8: Unspoken Truths

The next morning, Evelyn felt the weight of the previous day's encounter with Gabriel Stone pressing heavily on her. The photograph of the masked figures around the carousel haunted his thoughts. He had managed to stumble asleep, tossing and turning as the shadows of his past seemed to dance in the corners of his mind.

Determined to make progress, Evelyn decided to follow up on her request to review the records of the retreat. He arrived early at the retreat, with the fog floating over the gardens. The air was cold, and the fog gave the retreat an even more sinister atmosphere. She was greeted by Richard, who led her to a secure office where historical records were kept.

"This room contains all the archival materials from the early years of the retreat," Richard said, opening the door to a small, windowless room filled with filing cabinets and dusty boxes. "You'll have two hours to review the records. If you need anything, let me know."

Evelyn thanked him and began to review the documents. Most were mundane, detailing routine administrative matters and client records. However, upon digging deeper, he found a folder labeled "Historical Documents - Confidential." His heart raced as he opened it, revealing a collection of old reports, meeting minutes, and photographs.

One photograph immediately caught his eye: a group of people wearing ceremonial masks, similar to the one in the office photograph, standing around a carousel. The backdrop was unmistakably Whispering Pines. Next to it was a document detailing an annual event held by the retreat in the 1980s, described as a "cleansing ritual."

Evelyn's hands trembled as she continued reading. The documents described the Circle's ritual practices and its "purification ceremonies," which involved masked figures and haunting rites. The language was vague but chilling, hinting at psychological and physical abuse.

A sudden noise behind her made Evelyn jump. He turned and saw Daniel standing in the doorway, with a serious expression. "Dr. Caldwell, you seem to have discovered some sensitive material. I'm afraid you've run out of time.

Evelyn quickly gathered the documents and tried to memorize as much as she could. "I need more time. These records are crucial to understanding what happened here."

Daniel's expression remained stern. "I'm sorry, but the withdrawal policies are strict. You'll need to come back another time if you need more access."

As Daniel escorted her out of the office, Evelyn felt a twinge of frustration. He had barely scratched the surface of the truth. I needed to find another way to get the information I needed.

Back in her car, Evelyn noticed a familiar figure standing near the entrance to the retreat, the same man she had seen the day before. He watched her intently before diving back into the mist. Evelyn's instincts told her that she was being followed, but she couldn't be sure of the man's intentions.

Determined to face her fears, Evelyn decided to return to Whispering Pines that night. She wanted to visit the old house she and Diane had grown up in, hoping to find additional clues or memories.

The trip to Whispering Pines was tense. The fog seemed to thicken as night fell, enveloping the city in an eerie silence. The house stood before her, with the paint that had once been vibrant and the windows dark and desolate.

Evelyn approached the front door cautiously. It was locked, but he managed to enter through a window that he had left slightly ajar years ago. The interior was just as I remembered it: dusty and full of remnants of a past life. He moved through the rooms, each of which evoked memories of his childhood.

In the basement, he found an old trunk covered in dust. Inside were boxes with old photographs and personal belongings. Evelyn examined them carefully, looking for anything that might connect her mother to The Circle.

Among the objects, he found a small, ornate box. Inside were several old photographs of his mother with a group of people, all wearing masks. One photograph was particularly striking: his mother, young and frightened, standing next to Gabriel Stone. Evelyn's heart pounded as she realized the connection between her mother and Stone.

As she examined the photograph, a noise upstairs caused her to freeze. Someone was in the house. Evelyn's mind raced. She had to leave before she was caught. He quickly picked up the photographs and fled through the window, returning to his car.

The fog seemed even thicker on their way back, and the shadows of the trees seemed more threatening. Evelyn's thoughts were a whirlwind of fear and determination. He knew he was getting closer and closer to discovering the truth, but the dangers were becoming more real.

Arriving in Millbrook, Evelyn felt a mixture of relief and anxiety. She had uncovered crucial evidence, but the threat of persecution and the dangers she faced were becoming increasingly apparent. The next steps were clear: he needed to confront Gabriel Stone and discover the full extent of his involvement in The Circle.

Chapter 9: The Weight of Secrets

The next morning, Evelyn sat at the kitchen table, the photographs unfolded before her. He couldn't shake the image of his mother standing next to Gabriel Stone, his face was a mask of fear. The revelation felt like a heavy shroud around him, suffocating and unforgiving. Evelyn's mind raced as she tried to piece together the puzzle of her past.

His phone rang, breaking his concentration. It was a message from his sister, Diane: "We need to talk. It's about mom."

Evelyn's heart skipped a beat. The moment seemed too casual. She responded quickly, arranging a meet-and-greet with Diane at a local café. He knew that this conversation could shed more light on the mysterious connections between his family and The Circle.

At the café, Diane looked older and more worn than Evelyn remembered. They exchanged a tense hug before sitting down at a corner table. Diane's eyes were darkened with worry as she took a sip of her coffee.

"I saw your message," Diane began, her voice trembling. "I didn't want to dig up old wounds, but after seeing what you've discovered, I think we need to talk."

Evelyn nodded, her anxiety palpable. "I found a photograph of mom with Gabriel Stone. It was taken during what appears to be one of The Circle's rituals. I need to know what you remember about his participation.

Diane's face paled. "Mom was deeply involved with Stone and his group. She was one of his most devoted followers. I tried to stay away from their activities, but I knew enough to understand that they were dangerous."

Evelyn's mind raced. "Why didn't you tell me before? Why did you leave?"

Diane looked down at her hands, struggling to find the right words. "I was scared. I knew too much and I was afraid that if I talked, something bad would happen to me, or worse, to you. I thought moving was the best way to protect myself and my family."

Evelyn's frustration boiled over. "But this secret is what has kept us in the dark for so long! We have to face it head-on. If Stone is still involved with The Circle, we have to expose him."

Diane shook her head. "I understand your anger, but you don't know what you're dealing with. Gabriel Stone is dangerous. And The Circle is more powerful than you think. They have their hands in many places, including the police and local government."

Evelyn's heart sank. "What do you mean?" How far does its influence go?

Diane's voice was barely a whisper. "The mayor, police chief, and several other prominent figures in Whispering Pines have been involved with them. It is a network of power and control. Even if you find out the truth, they will try to silence you."

Evelyn took a deep breath, feeling the weight of Diane's words. "I have to continue. I have to uncover the truth and bring it to light, no matter the risk."

Diane looked at her with a mixture of fear and determination. "If you're on this path, you need to be careful. You can't trust anyone. And remember, you're not alone. I'll help you in any way I can, but you have to be cautious."

As they parted, Evelyn felt a renewed sense of determination. Diane's information about the extent of The Circle's influence made the situation even more dangerous. I knew I had to tread carefully, but now I couldn't turn back.

Back at home, Evelyn tried to focus on her next steps. He decided to dig deeper into Gabriel Stone's background and the retirement's connections to local officials. Her research led her to discover that Stone had been involved in several community projects and had connections to high-profile people in Millbrook.

As night fell, Evelyn noticed a shadow moving outside her window. His heart raced as he peered through the blinds and saw the same man from the retreat guarding his house. She felt a shiver of paranoia and knew she had to be alert.

He quickly closed the doors and windows, and then began gathering his findings in a secure folder. She needed to be prepared for anything, including the possibility of her home being broken into. Evelyn considered asking Detective Holloway for help, but hesitated, unsure if she could trust him given the web of deception she was unraveling.

The day had taken its toll on him, and as he lay in bed, the events of the day were playing out in his mind. The photograph, Diane's revelations, and the watchman's ominous presence outside all contributed to a sense of imminent danger.

Evelyn decided to meet with Holloway the next day, hoping that he might be able to provide some help or at least offer some protection. She couldn't shake the feeling that the walls were closing, but she was determined to face whatever came next.

Chapter 10: The Unraveling Net

Evelyn awoke with a start, her dreams filled with fragmented memories and shadows of The Circle. Scarcely had he slept, his mind racing with thoughts of Gabriel Stone and the extent of his influence. Determined to make progress, she prepared to meet with Detective Holloway, hoping that he might shed light on the connections between the recent murders and her own past.

He arrived at the police station early, his heart pounding with anxiety. Detective Holloway was already at his desk, examining the files. He looked up as Evelyn entered, with an expression of curiosity and caution.

"Dr. Caldwell, get there early," he said, beckoning her to sit down. "What do you have for me today?"

Evelyn took a deep breath, trying to calm her nerves. "I have discovered disturbing information about Gabriel Stone and his involvement in The Circle. I need your help to understand the connections between him, the murders and the influence of this group."

Holloway's interest was piqued as he leaned forward. "Go on.

Evelyn placed the photographs and documents she had gathered on her desk. "These are documents of Stone's retirement. They indicate that El Círculo never dissolved. Instead, its members have been integrated into positions of power. I also found a photograph of my mother with Stone and other members of The Circle."

Holloway examined the documents closely. "This is serious. If what you say is true, it means that we are dealing with a much bigger conspiracy than we initially thought."

Evelyn nodded. "Yes, and I am concerned about the connections between El Círculo and local officials. Diane, my sister, mentioned that several prominent figures from Whispering Pines are involved with them. That includes the mayor and the police chief."

Holloway's expression darkened. "I have noticed some irregularities in the cases I am investigating. Some of the victims had connections to Whispering Pines, and the details seem to line up with what you're describing. I need to deepen these links, but if there is corruption at higher levels, things get complicated."

Evelyn's anxiety grew. "What should I do now? I feel like I'm being watched and I fear for my safety."

Holloway considered his words carefully. "We will have to be cautious. I can offer you some protection, but it won't be easy. I'll also need to verify your information discreetly. If we're dealing with a network of powerful individuals, we have to be strategic."

Evelyn agreed, feeling a mixture of relief and apprehension. "Thank you, detective." I appreciate your help."

As Evelyn left the station, she felt a glimmer of hope that Holloway's involvement could make a difference. However, he was also well aware of the dangers that lay ahead.

The rest of the day passed in a hazy activity as Evelyn continued her investigation. He combed through old newspaper articles and public records related to Gabriel Stone and The Circle, trying to find any additional evidence that might support his claims. The more she discovered, the more she realized how deeply ingrained The Circle was in the fabric of the community.

Late in the afternoon, while Evelyn was reviewing her notes, she received a call from Diane. His voice was tense and urgent. "Evelyn, I've been doing some digging on my own. I found something you have to see: an old diary that belonged to Mom. I could have more information about his participation in The Circle."

Evelyn's heart raced. "Where is it?"

Diane provided an address for a small storage unit that she had kept hidden for years. Evelyn thanked him and headed for the place, her mind overflowing with anticipation and fear.

The storage room was located on the outskirts of the city. Evelyn opened it and opened the door carefully. Inside, he found an assortment of old boxes and furniture. Diane's diary was in a dusty box with the inscription "Personal."

Evelyn opened the diary and began to read. The entries were fragmented, but revealed disturbing details about her mother's life and her relationship with Gabriel Stone. The diary described secret meetings, rituals, and the growing influence of The Circle. Evelyn's mother had been deeply involved in planning the group's activities and keeping it secret.

One entry stood out: "Tonight's ceremony is crucial. Gabriel is pushing for a bigger role in the community. We must ensure that our influence remains hidden as we expand our reach."

The words sent a shiver down Evelyn's spine. Her mother had been more than just a participant: she had been a key figure in the group's operations.

When Evelyn closed the diary, she felt a sense of determination. The evidence was piling up and the truth was at hand. He needed to stand up to Gabriel Stone and expose the corruption of The Circle before it was too late.

With renewed determination, Evelyn returned to Millbrook, ready to face any challenge that came her way. The web of deception was crumbling, and she was at the center of it, struggling to bring the truth to light.

Chapter 11: In the Shadows

Evelyn's determination was matched only by her growing sense of unease. The newspaper's revelations about his mother's involvement in The Circle weighed heavily on his mind. He knew he had to act quickly to prevent further damage, but the web of deception seemed to be tightening around him.

He spent the night reviewing his notes and planning his next steps. With the magazine's new evidence, its focus shifted to Gabriel Stone's wellness retreat. The retreat, which was supposed to be a place of healing, now appeared to be the epicenter of the ongoing conspiracy.

The next morning, Evelyn drove to the retreat location, a secluded property outside of Whispering Pines. The retreat was set in a picturesque setting with sprawling grounds and serene surroundings, a stark contrast to the sinister activities rumored to be taking place there.

As Evelyn approached the entrance, she took a deep breath and steeled herself. He needed to gather more evidence, and the best way to do that was to mingle and observe. She had prepared a cover story: she was interested in the services of the retreat for her own personal well-being.

The receptionist greeted her with a warm smile and Evelyn introduced herself. "Hi, I'm Dr. Evelyn Caldwell. I'm interested in learning more about their retirement and the programs they offer."

The receptionist's smile widened. "Welcome, Dr. Caldwell. We offer a variety of programs designed to promote holistic healing and personal growth. Gabriel Stone himself conducts many of the sessions. I can arrange a meeting for you."

Evelyn felt a twinge of apprehension, but she kept her composure. "That would be great. I would like to speak with Mr. Stone about his approach and how it could benefit me."

While waiting for her date with Stone, Evelyn wandered around the grounds of the retreat. The atmosphere was meticulously maintained and the atmosphere was serene, almost idyllic. However, he couldn't shake the feeling that something was lurking beneath the surface.

His thoughts were interrupted by a gentle tap on his shoulder. Evelyn turned around and found a young woman standing in front of her. He had a kind face and an air of quiet confidence. "You must be Dr. Caldwell," said the woman. "I'm Lila Matthews. I've heard about your interest in retirement."

Evelyn's heart skipped a beat. Lila's presence here was unexpected and unsettling. "Yes, I'm here to learn more about what they offer. Are you a participant here?"

Lila nodded. "I've been here for a while. It's been... enlightening. Gabriel Stone is an extraordinary person. I'm sure his approach will be quite transformative."

Evelyn tried to read Lila's expression, looking for any hint of the fear or distress she had shown during her sessions. Lila's demeanor was calm and collected, but there was an unsettling tone to her words.

Their conversation was interrupted when the receptionist reappeared, indicating that Gabriel Stone was ready to see Evelyn. Lila wished him well and left, leaving Evelyn alone to confront Stone.

Gabriel Stone's office was a serene space with large windows overlooking the retirement grounds. The room was decorated with soothing colors and soft furnishings, designed to evoke a sense of tranquility. Stone himself was a charismatic figure, exuding a magnetic presence.

"Dr. Caldwell, it's nice to meet you," Stone said, holding out his hand. "I understand that you are interested in learning more about our retirement."

Evelyn shook his hand firmly, maintaining her professional demeanor. "Yes, Mr. Stone. I've heard a lot about your work and I wanted to understand your approach to healing and personal growth."

Stone motioned for her to sit down. "Our approach is unique. We believe in addressing the whole person: mind, body, and spirit. Our programs are designed to help people connect with their true selves and overcome the barriers that hold them back."

As Stone spoke, Evelyn listened intently, trying to discern any hints of deception or ulterior motives. He highlighted the way he spoke with such conviction and how he framed his words to emphasize the transformative nature of his programs.

"I'm particularly interested in understanding more about the group sessions they offer," Evelyn said, carefully phrasing her question. "What can participants expect from these experiences?"

Stone's eyes shone with excitement. "Our group sessions are designed to foster a deep sense of connection and self-discovery. Participants participate in various exercises and discussions that help them discover hidden aspects of themselves and release emotional blockages. It's a powerful process."

Evelyn nodded, noding the careful choice of words. "That sounds intriguing. I'm curious what types of exercises you use and how they're designed to achieve these results."

Stone smiled warmly. "We use a variety of techniques, including guided meditations, reflective exercises, and group dialogues. Each activity is designed to support personal growth and healing. I think you'll find the experience to be both enlightening and empowering."

Their conversation continued for another hour, during which Stone shared more details about the retreat's programs and philosophy. Evelyn remained vigilant, taking mental notes of any discrepancies or suspicious behavior.

At the conclusion of the meeting, Evelyn thanked Stone and left her office. He felt a mixture of restlessness and determination. Stone's charisma and the serene atmosphere of the retreat masked a deeper, more problematic reality.

Back in her car, Evelyn reviewed the information she had gathered. He needed to remain vigilant and gather more evidence to expose the truth about The Circle and its influence. The retreat might contain more secrets, and she was determined to uncover them.

As she walked away from the retreat, Evelyn couldn't shake the feeling that she was being watched. His paranoia grew, but he knew he had to move on. The truth was within her grasp, and she was determined to carry it out, no matter the personal cost.

Chapter 12: The Hidden Layers

Evelyn realized that the charm of the retreat was a carefully constructed façade. The more I learned, the more evident it became that beneath the surface of serenity and self-improvement was a web of deception and manipulation. The diary, the atmosphere of the retreat, and Stone's charisma were pieces of a complex puzzle that Evelyn was determined to solve.

The next day, Evelyn returned to Millbrook with a renewed sense of urgency. He needed to dig deeper into Stone's connections and uncover more evidence of The Circle's operations. The information he had gathered so far was disturbing, but it was not enough to expose the full extent of the conspiracy.

He headed straight to his office, where he could work in relative privacy. His first task was to review the images from the security cameras in his office. After Lila's unexpected appearance at the retreat, Evelyn felt it was crucial to understand how her behavior had changed since her last session. He hoped to find clues that could reveal more about Lila's current state of mind.

As Evelyn reviewed the footage, she saw Lila drifting in and out of her office several times, each visit marked by a growing sense of urgency. Lila's behavior had gone from fragile and distressed to calm and collected. Evelyn noticed the change, but she still couldn't discern its meaning.

He then turned his attention to the retreat's online presence, looking for reviews or testimonials that could shed light on his operations. The retreat website was full of enthusiastic endorsements, but Evelyn knew not to take them at face value. He found some negative reviews buried deep in the site's archives, reviews that spoke of disappointment and dissatisfaction, but were vague and lacked specific details.

Determined to dig deeper, Evelyn decided to visit the local library to research the history of the retreat and its founder. I hoped to find any records or articles that could provide insight into Stone's past and the origins of The Circle.

In the library, Evelyn pored over old newspaper clippings and public records. He found several articles on Gabriel Stone's rise to prominence and the establishment of his retirement. Articles praised his innovative approach to holistic healing, but lacked any critical examination. Evelyn's frustration grew when she realized that the media coverage had been overwhelmingly positive, likely due to Stone's influence and connections.

His breakthrough came when he discovered a series of articles from decades ago, before Stone's rise to fame. These articles covered a series of mysterious disappearances at Whispering Pines, disappearances that coincided with the early years of The Circle's activities. The cases were never solved, but the patterns were striking. All of the victims had been prominent figures in the community, and their disappearances were shrouded in secrecy.

Evelyn's heart raced as she read the articles. The connections between the disappearances and El Círculo were becoming clearer and clearer. It seemed that Stone and his associates had been operating in the shadows for much longer than she had initially imagined.

As she left the library, Evelyn felt a sense of urgency. He needed to stand up to Stone and expose the truth before any more damage could be done. But first, he needed to gather additional evidence to back up his claims.

Back in her office, Evelyn found a letter slipped under her door. It was an anonymous note with a chilling message: "The carousel never stops spinning. Be careful, or you could become the next player."

The message sent shivers down her spine. The phrase was a direct reference to the one Lila had uttered during her first session. Evelyn knew she was about to discover something important, but she also realized that the danger was increasing.

He decided to contact Detective Holloway and update him on his findings. They needed to coordinate their efforts and make sure they were prepared for what lay ahead.

Holloway agreed to meet her at a nearby café. As they sat down, Evelyn shared her recent discoveries and the anonymous note. Holloway listened intently, his expression growing more serious with each passing moment.

"This is more than a case of corruption or fraud," Holloway said, quietly. "We are dealing with a deep-seated conspiracy that has been operating for decades. The connections between The Circle, Stone and the disappearances are troubling."

Evelyn nodded. "Yes, and I'm worried that we're running out of time. The Circle's influence is very wide, and they are not afraid to use violence to protect their secrets."

Holloway agreed. "I will start digging into the old cases and see if we can find any link between the disappearances and the current killings. We have to be cautious and gather as much evidence as possible."

As she left the café, Evelyn felt a renewed sense of determination. The pieces of the puzzle were beginning to fall into place, but the full picture was still elusive. He knew that uncovering the truth would require more than investigation: it would require courage and resilience in the face of growing danger.

With her determination solidified, Evelyn prepared for the next phase of her investigation. She was ready to confront the darkness that had dogged her past and bring to light the sinister operations of The Circle.

Chapter 13: The Edge of Revelation

The sun had barely risen when Evelyn returned to Whispering Pines. The city seemed eerily quiet, as if holding its breath, anticipating the chaos that was about to unfold. His concentration was sharp; he needed to access the inner workings of the retreat and further investigate Stone's connections. The note he received only added to his sense of urgency.

He approached retirement with a new sense of determination. His previous visit had been a reconnaissance mission; Today, I intended to dig deeper. Evelyn decided to try a different approach: She would attend one of the group sessions Stone had mentioned to see firsthand what was happening behind closed doors.

The receptionist greeted her with the same warm smile. "Good morning, Dr. Caldwell. Ready for your session?"

"Yes," Evelyn replied, trying to mask her anxiety with a professional attitude. "I can't wait to experience the show and see what it has to offer."

The receptionist led her to a large, airy room where she was about to start a group session. The room was decorated with soothing colors and soft lighting, designed to create a tranquil atmosphere. The participants were already seated in a circle, their faces reflecting a range of emotions, from anticipation to apprehension.

Evelyn took her place in the circle, trying to blend in. He observed the behavior of the participants: some were visibly nervous, while others seemed eerily serene. He recognized some faces from the retreat's promotional material and wondered about their true experiences.

As the session began, Gabriel Stone entered the room, radiating an aura of authority and calm. He greeted everyone with a warm, inviting smile and began to speak in a reassuring tone. "Welcome everyone. Today, we will explore the concept of personal transformation and how it relates to our inner selves. We will use guided meditation to delve into our subconscious and uncover hidden truths."

Evelyn watched closely as Stone led the group through a series of relaxation exercises. His voice was hypnotic, guiding the participants into a state of deep relaxation. The room was filled with the soft hum of ambient music, creating a surreal atmosphere.

During the meditation, Evelyn's mind was alert, carefully analyzing every detail. He noticed the subtle manipulation techniques Stone employed: his language was designed to elicit emotional responses and make participants vulnerable. It was clear that his methods were more than just therapeutic; They were manipulative and insidious.

After the session, Evelyn mingled with the other participants, trying to gather more information. He approached a woman named Sarah, who seemed particularly distressed during the session. "Hi, I'm Dr. Caldwell. How was the session for you?

Sarah looked at Evelyn with wary eyes. "It was intense. I'm not sure if I'm ready to face some of the things that came up."

Evelyn nodded sympathetically. "It can be overwhelming. Have you been attending these sessions for a long time?"

Sarah hesitated before answering. "A few months. I was drawn here by personal growth, but lately I've been feeling more confused than ever. There's something about the way things are handled here that doesn't sit well with me."

Evelyn's curiosity was piqued. "What do you mean?"

Sarah looked around nervously before continuing. "There's a lot of pressure to conform, and some of the activities feel more like rituals than therapy. I've been thinking about leaving, but I'm afraid of the repercussions."

The conversation was abruptly interrupted as Stone approached, narrowing his eyes slightly. "Dr. Caldwell, I hope you find the sessions beneficial."

Evelyn forced a smile. "Yes, thank you. I'm gaining valuable information."

Stone's gaze rested on her for a moment longer before he excused himself to attend to other business. Evelyn watched him go, her mind racing. Sarah's comments confirmed her suspicions about the true nature of the retreat.

As Evelyn prepared to leave, she sensed a subtle change in the atmosphere. The retreat staff seemed to be watching her more closely, their smiles now tinged with a hint of suspicion. Evelyn realized that his presence was no longer as low-key as she had hoped.

He decided it was time to regroup and review his findings. He came out of retirement with a growing sense of urgency and a determination to expose the truth. Their next step was to find more concrete evidence linking Stone and The Circle to recent murders and disappearances in the past.

Back in Millbrook, Evelyn met with Detective Holloway to share her latest observations. They talked about the breakout session and Sarah's concerns, which only added weight to their research. Holloway promised to follow up on the information and see if there was any connection to the murder cases.

On leaving the police station, Evelyn received another anonymous note. This one was more cryptic: "Masks are more than just symbols. They hide the true face of evil."

The note sent shivers down her spine. It was clear that whoever was behind these messages was watching her closely and trying to intimidate her into backing down. But Evelyn's determination was unwavering. He knew that exposing the dark secrets of The Circle was not just a personal mission, but a moral imperative.

She returned to her office, determined to piece together the remaining pieces of the puzzle. The danger was mounting, but Evelyn was prepared to face what was coming. The road to the truth was fraught with danger, but she was ready to face it, no matter the cost.

Chapter 14: The Unexpected Ally

Evelyn's journey back to Whispering Pines was fraught with tension. The insidious atmosphere of the retreat had left her uneasy, and the anonymous notes added to her sense of dread. He needed to act quickly and decisively to unravel the truth about Gabriel Stone and The Circle.

The night was settling down when Evelyn arrived at her sister Diane's house. The small, modest home contrasted with the opulence of Stone's retreat, but it exuded a warmth that Evelyn found comforting. Diane greeted her with a mixture of surprise and concern.

"Evelyn, what's going on? You seemed so urgent on the phone," Diane asked, leading her into the living room.

Evelyn sat down, her expression serious. "I have discovered disturbing information about Gabriel Stone and retirement. I think it's connected to The Circle and the disappearances of our childhood. I need your help."

Diane's face paled. "I've been trying to avoid all of this for years. I thought we had left it behind."

"I know," Evelyn said quietly, "but I can't do this alone. The retreat is more than a façade; It's a place where terrible things are happening. I need to understand our past and his connection to Stone."

Diane hesitated, but finally nodded. "Very good. What do you need from me?

Evelyn took a deep breath. "I need to have access to any old records or documents about our mother and Gabriel Stone. Anything that can provide a link between them and The Circle."

Diane nodded and took Evelyn to a small study in the back of the house. He pulled an old box out of a closet, filled with papers, photographs, and faded letters. Evelyn sifted through the contents, her heart racing as she searched for anything that might shed light on her mother's relationship with Stone.

While Evelyn was examining the documents, she found several letters between her mother and Stone. The letters were filled with references to gatherings, rituals, and a shared vision of a new community. The language was cryptic, but the context was alarming. It became clear that her mother had been deeply involved with Stone and The Circle.

Among the papers, Evelyn also discovered a photograph of a group gathering, with Stone in the center, surrounded by masked figures. The photo dated from the early days of The Circle, and Evelyn's mother was standing next to Stone, with a look of intense devotion on her face.

"That's all," Evelyn said, holding up the photograph. "This is proof of their participation. It's exactly what I needed."

Diane looked worried. "But what do we do with this information? How do we expose them?"

"We must take him to Detective Holloway," Evelyn said. "He has been investigating the murders, and this could be the breakthrough he needs. We also have to be careful. The Circle is dangerous, and they won't be happy with us discovering its secrets.

Diane agreed, and they decided to meet with Holloway the next morning. Evelyn spent the rest of the night organizing the documents and preparing a summary of her findings. Diane offered her support, but it was clear that she was also deeply affected by the revelations.

The next morning, Evelyn and Diane arrived at the police station. Holloway greeted them with a mixture of curiosity and concern.

"I have something important to show you," Evelyn said, handing him the documents and the photograph.

Holloway reviewed the materials with intense scrutiny. "This is significant. It's clear that Stone was involved with The Circle from the beginning. We need to verify these documents and see if we can find any corroborating evidence."

Evelyn nodded. "I will help in any way I can. I also have a clue about some of the retreat activities that could provide more information."

Holloway's expression was resolute. "We will proceed carefully. This case is taking a dangerous turn and we have to be prepared for anything."

As she left the station, Evelyn felt a sense of cautious optimism. The documents and photograph were crucial evidence, but the real challenge was to uncover the full extent of The Circle's operations and ensure justice for the victims.

Diane, though visibly shaken, had become an unexpected ally in Evelyn's search for the truth. Their support was invaluable and Evelyn was grateful for their help.

As Evelyn prepared for the next steps in her investigation, she knew that the road ahead would be fraught with danger. The Circle's influence was far-reaching, and it was unlikely that they would relinquish their control without a fight. But with the new evidence in hand and Holloway's support, Evelyn felt a renewed sense of purpose. The battle against The Circle was far from over, but she was determined to see it through to the end.

Chapter 15: The Deepest Shadows

The following days were a whirlwind of activity. Detective Holloway had taken the newly discovered evidence seriously and had begun the process of corroborating the documents and photograph. Evelyn, meanwhile, was on high alert, her days full of preparation and her nights haunted by vivid nightmares of masked figures and sinister rituals.

Diane had reluctantly returned to her routine, but she was still a vital part of Evelyn's support network. The sisters had grown closer through the ordeal, their shared history, and the trauma of their past, creating a bond that was both painful and empowering.

One night, while Evelyn was sitting in her office, she received an unexpected phone call. It was Sarah, the retreat participant, who had voiced her concerns. His voice was tinged with panic.

"Dr. Caldwell, I need your help. I've been trying to come out of retirement, but they're making it impossible for me. They are watching me and I don't know who to trust."

Evelyn's heart raced. "Calm down, Sarah. What's going on? Why can't you leave?"

"They have closed the doors. They say it's part of the process, but I know it's a control tactic. They've been pressuring us to share our deepest secrets, and I'm afraid they're using it to blackmail us or worse," Sarah explained, her voice trembling.

Evelyn could hear the desperation in Sarah's tone. "I'll come and see you. I have some information about The Circle, and I think we can use it to get you out of there. Stay calm and try to keep a low profile."

Evelyn met with Holloway to inform him about the situation. He was worried, but agreed that they needed to act quickly. He suggested that they prepare a plan to rescue Sarah and gather more evidence against Stone and The Circle.

Under cover of darkness, Evelyn and Holloway approached the retreat. They parked a few blocks away and discreetly approached the building. Holloway had arranged a small team of officers to assist with the operation.

Evelyn's heart pounded with every step, her mind racing with thoughts of what might be to come.

Once inside, they navigated the labyrinthine corridors of the retreat. The place was eerily quiet, the only sounds being the faint hum of the air conditioner and the distant murmur of voices. Evelyn took Holloway to the area where she believed Sarah was being held.

Upon reaching the door of the restricted zone, Evelyn's pulse accelerated. He noticed that there was a security camera mounted overhead, with the red light flashing constantly. They had to be cautious; Any sign of intrusion could jeopardize their mission.

Holloway signaled to his team, and they quickly turned off the camera. They opened the door carefully and entered, moving silently to avoid detection. Evelyn and Holloway's breaths came in shallow gasps as they approached the room where Sarah was being held.

They found Sara sitting on a small cot, her eyes wide with fear. "Dr. Caldwell!" he exclaimed, running to the door.

Evelyn ran to her, opening the door with a spare key they had obtained. "We're here to get you out. Stay close and follow us."

As they returned through the retreat, Evelyn and Holloway's nerves were on edge. They had to navigate the labyrinthine design of the building while avoiding detection. The retreat staff were suspiciously absent, but Evelyn had no doubt that her escape would soon be noticed.

Just as they approached the exit, a voice crackled over the intercom. "Attention, all the staff. We have a security breach. Close the facilities immediately."

The announcement caused a wave of panic in Evelyn. They were running out of time. Holloway urged everyone to move faster, and they ran for the exit. The security team of the retreat was approaching and the situation was becoming more and more serious.

As they burst through the exit and into the night, Evelyn's heart sank. They had succeeded, but their troubles were far from over. The retreat staff would be looking for them, and The Circle's reach was extensive.

Back in the safety of their office, Evelyn and Holloway questioned Sarah and reviewed the information they had gathered. Sarah's testimony added crucial details about the methods of the retreat and the psychological manipulation used by Stone and his associates.

Evelyn felt a growing sense of urgency. The retreat was only one piece of the puzzle, and they needed to keep moving forward to expose the full extent of The Circle's operations. With Sarah's help and Holloway's continued support, Evelyn was determined to bring the truth to light and end The Circle's reign of terror.

Chapter 16: The Web Tightens

The days that followed Sarah's rescue were tense but productive. Evelyn and Detective Holloway worked tirelessly to piece together the evidence they had gathered. The retreat was under investigation, but the Circle's influence and the extent of its operations remained hidden.

Evelyn's office was a makeshift command center. The walls were covered with photographs, documents, and maps, all connected by threads of red thread. It was a visual representation of the complex web of connections that Evelyn and Holloway were trying to unravel.

One night, while Evelyn was reviewing the latest reports, Holloway arrived with an update. His expression was gloomy and he was carrying a thick folder.

"We've made some progress," he said, setting the folder down on the desk. "We've cross-referenced the documents he provided with other records and found some disturbing links."

Evelyn's curiosity was piqued. "What did you find?"

Holloway flipped through the folder and pulled out a series of photographs and documents. "These are records of people who were part of El Círculo but who have since assumed prominent positions in various sectors. We're talking about politicians, business leaders, and even some law enforcement officials."

Evelyn scanned the documents. The names and faces were familiar to him, people he had heard about in the media or seen in passing. Realizing this hit her hard. The Circle was not just a local problem; it was ingrained in the fabric of society.

"There's more," Holloway continued. "We have identified a pattern of cover-up and obstruction of justice. It seems that El Círculo has been manipulating and controlling people from behind the scenes for years."

Evelyn's mind raced. "If they are so deeply ingrained, how can we expect to expose them?"

"We're not alone in this," Holloway said. "I've been in contact with some trusted colleagues and other law enforcement agencies. We need to build a coalition to confront this head-on."

While discussing their next steps, Evelyn received a call from Diane. Her voice was trembling and she was clearly annoyed. "Evelyn, I just received a threatening note. It's similar to the ones you've been getting."

Evelyn's heart sank. "What did it say?"

Diane's voice trembled. "He mentioned The Circle and warned me to stay away from his business if he valued my safety."

Evelyn's mind was racing with worry. "Take care, Diane. Don't leave the house until I can get to you.

Evelyn and Holloway made their way to Diane's house. The atmosphere was full of tension upon his arrival. Diane was visibly shaken, but she tried to keep her composure.

"This note slipped under my door," Diane said, handing him a folded piece of paper. The message was clear and threatening: *Your meddling will not be tolerated. Leave the past buried or face the consequences.*"

Holloway took the note and examined it. "This confirms that El Círculo is monitoring us closely. We have to be cautious and keep our movements discreet."

Evelyn agreed. "We need to accelerate our efforts. If they are making threats, it means that they are feeling the pressure. We must use this to our advantage."

In the days that followed, Evelyn, Holloway, and their trusted allies worked in secret. They coordinated efforts to gather more evidence and identify key players within The Circle. The investigation was coming to a head and the danger was growing.

As Evelyn delved deeper into the investigation, she discovered disturbing information about the connections between The Circle and some of her own acquaintances. The realization that people he had once trusted might be involved in the conspiracy was deeply disturbing.

Despite mounting pressure and threats, Evelyn's resolve remained unwavering. She was determined to carry out the investigation and bring The Circle to justice. The web of deception was tightening, but Evelyn was more determined than ever to expose the truth and dismantle the sinister organization that had plagued her life and the lives of many others.

Chapter 17: The Price of Truth

The sun had barely risen when Evelyn and Holloway arrived at the library in downtown Millbrook. It was his designated meeting point with Sarah and some trusted law enforcement allies who had been briefed on his investigation. Evelyn's nerves were on edge, but her determination was unwavering.

Inside the library, a quiet urgency filled the air as they gathered around a large table in a secluded corner. Sara arrived, anxious but determined. Holloway introduced him to the new allies: Officer Jenna Marks, an experienced investigator with a keen eye for detail, and Frank Donovan, a private investigator with connections to several underground networks.

Evelyn wasted no time in informing everyone about her recent findings and outlining her next steps. "We have uncovered significant evidence linking The Circle to several influential figures. Our immediate goal is to secure this evidence and make sure it gets to the proper authorities."

Sarah nodded, her face pale but determined. "I have managed to gather additional information from my time in retirement. There is a hidden ledger that details the transactions and activities related to The Circle's operations. It is kept in a safe area within the retreat."

Frank Donovan leaned forward. "If we can get our hands on that ledger, it could be the smoking gun we need. But we need a plan to access it without getting caught."

Holloway's eyes were sharp. "We have already established vigilance in the withdrawal, but we need to increase our efforts. We should coordinate with Frank's contacts and come up with a strategy to get in and out without drawing attention to ourselves.

As they discussed the details of their plan, Evelyn's phone rang with a message. It was Diane's, who had been staying at a friend's house for safety. The message was brief but alarming: *"There has been a robbery. They didn't take anything, but they left a message on the wall. Be careful."*

Evelyn's heart pounded as she relayed the information. "We have to be very cautious. The Circle is not only watching us, but is actively trying to intimidate us."

Officer Marks nodded. "We must increase patrols around Diane's location and make sure she is safe. In the meantime, let's focus on securing the ledger."

The team split up, and Sarah and Evelyn headed to the retreat to retrieve the ledger, while Holloway, Marks, and Donovan worked to bolster their surveillance and security measures.

Undercover and well prepared, Evelyn and Sarah approached the retreat late at night. They used a set of stolen access codes to bypass the security system, their movements synchronized and precise. The retreat was eerily quiet, the only sounds being their cautious footsteps and the distant hum of machinery.

They made their way through the dark corridors, their lanterns casting long shadows on the walls. Evelyn's heart raced as they reached the safe zone where the ledger was kept. Sarah knew the design well and guided Evelyn into the room with the hidden vault.

With trembling hands, Sarah struggled to bypass the combination lock. Evelyn kept a watchful eye, every crack and whisper sending a shiver down her spine. After a few tense minutes, the lock opened, revealing a small safe inside.

Sarah's hands were steady as she picked up the ledger. It was a heavy, leather-bound book full of detailed records. Evelyn carefully removed it, her relief palpable but short-lived. They still had to escape.

Just as they were about to leave, a sudden noise echoed in the retreat. The footsteps and voices grew louder, indicating that their presence had been detected. Evelyn's stomach knotted when she realized that they were running out of time.

They hurried back through the corridors, their escape becoming more and more urgent. The tension was palpable as they turned corners and hid in the shadows, trying to avoid detection. Evelyn's mind raced with thoughts of what would happen if they were caught.

Finally, they reached the exit and burst into the cool night air. They ran to their vehicle, the weight of the ledger a constant reminder of the danger they had narrowly escaped. Evelyn and Sarah exchanged looks of relief as they drove away from the retreat, their adrenaline slowly fading.

Back at Evelyn's office, Holloway, Marks, and Donovan were waiting. Evelyn handed over the ledger and the group began to review its contents. The ledger was filled with incriminating evidence: transactions, names, and detailed records of The Circle's activities.

The discovery was a breakthrough, but Evelyn knew her work was far from over. The influence of the Circle was still strong, and they had to be prepared for what might come next. As they continued to analyze the evidence, Evelyn felt a renewed sense of determination. The fight against The Circle was coming to a head, and she was ready to see it through to the end.

Chapter 18: The Unraveling Truth

Dawn broke over Millbrook, casting a pale light through the windows of Evelyn's office. The team had worked through the night, reviewing the contents of the ledger. As exhaustion gripped them, they knew they were on the verge of a breakthrough.

Evelyn rubbed her eyes and took a deep breath. The ledger had confirmed many of his suspicions, but it also introduced new questions. Key figures within The Circle had been documented, and their influence extended far beyond what they had imagined.

Holloway sat across from Evelyn, his face scarred with concern. "We have a lot of work ahead of us. This ledger is a gold mine, but it's also a big risk. If The Circle realizes we have it, we could be in even greater danger."

Evelyn nodded, feeling the weight of responsibility. "We have to carefully select the information we publish. It has to be strategically filtered to ensure it reaches the right people without compromising our security."

At that moment, Sarah entered the room, with a grim expression. "I've been going through the financial records of the general ledger. There are significant payments to several shell companies, and many of them are linked to prominent public figures."

Frank Donovan, who had been reviewing the names on the ledger, added: "I recognise some of these names. They are connected to local politicians and business leaders who have been involved in shady business dealings for years. The influence of the Circle is even more extensive than we thought."

Holloway frowned. "If we can prove these connections, we could expose The Circle's network and dismantle its operations. But you have to be careful. The higher corruption goes, the more dangerous it becomes."

Evelyn agreed. "We need to create a detailed report and coordinate with trusted journalists and law enforcement officials. They can help us spread the word while protecting our identities."

The team worked diligently to compile the evidence into a comprehensive report. They cross-referenced the details of the ledger with public records and previous investigations. The connections they uncovered painted a disturbing picture of corruption and manipulation.

Meanwhile, Evelyn couldn't shake the feeling that they were being watched. Strange occurrences (a shadowy figure following his car, anonymous phone calls) suggested that The Circle was aware of his activities. The paranoia was palpable, but Evelyn tried to stay focused.

Late in the evening, as Evelyn prepared to leave the office, Holloway approached her with a worried expression. "We have a problem. There has been an attempt to breach our security. Someone tried to access the server where we were storing the report."

Evelyn's heart raced. "What do we do?"

"We need to move the information immediately and make sure our digital footprint is secure," Holloway said. "I will coordinate with technology experts to manage the gap."

Sarah chimed in: "We should also consider making a partial release public. It could force The Circle to act prematurely, giving us a chance to be one step ahead."

Evelyn nodded. "Let's write a press release describing the main findings without giving too many details. We need to find a balance between exposing the truth and protecting our sources."

As the team worked through the night on the press release and security measures, the tension was palpable. They knew their actions could trigger a response from The Circle, but they were committed to carrying out the investigation.

By morning, they had prepared the press release and secured their digital files. The report was sent to trusted journalists with instructions to initially publish only parts of it. The hope was that this would spark public interest and put pressure on the authorities to take action.

Evelyn felt a mixture of relief and anxiety. They had taken an important step, but the danger was far from over. The Circle was likely to retaliate, and the team needed to remain vigilant.

When Evelyn and her team saw the first news about the investigation begin to circulate, they knew they had unleashed a firestorm. The truth that was unraveling was out there, and it was only a matter of time before the dark secrets of The Circle came to light. The fight was far from over, but Evelyn was ready to face any challenge that came her way.

Chapter 19: The Hidden Camera

The town of Millbrook was abuzz with the revelations of the partial report, and media coverage had reached a fever pitch. Public outrage was growing, and it seemed that El Círculo was struggling to contain the consequences. Evelyn could feel a change in the air, but she knew that the most dangerous part of her journey was yet to come.

In the quiet of her home, Evelyn sat at the dining room table with Holloway and Sarah, reviewing the latest updates and planning her next moves. The tension was palpable as they considered their options.

Holloway's phone rang with a new alert. "There has been a sighting of someone who looks like a key figure in The Circle. I've traced the trail to an abandoned warehouse on the outskirts of Millbrook."

Evelyn's heart skipped a beat. "If El Círculo is operating from there, it could be their new base of operations. We need to investigate immediately."

Sarah nodded, her expression determined. "We have to be cautious. If they're so desperate, they could be more dangerous than ever."

The team prepared for their reconnaissance mission, assembling teams and revising their plans. Evelyn couldn't shake the sense of imminent danger, but she was driven by a fierce determination to uncover the truth.

They arrived at the warehouse just as it was beginning to get dark. The building was a dilapidated structure, with broken windows and rusted metal doors suggesting years of neglect. Holloway led the way, his flashlight cutting through the encroaching darkness.

Evelyn, Sarah, and Holloway moved stealthily through the warehouse, their steps muffled by layers of dust and debris. The building was eerily quiet, adding to the tension of their search.

As they explored the warehouse, they came across a hidden door, barely noticeable against the wall. It was partially hidden by piles of old boxes and cobwebs. Evelyn's heart raced as she examined the door, her instincts telling her it was something meaningful.

With Holloway's help, they opened the door, revealing a narrow staircase that led into darkness. The air grew colder as they descended, and the sense of foreboding grew stronger.

At the bottom of the stairs, they found themselves in a dimly lit chamber. The room was filled with strange artifacts and symbols, the meaning of which was unknown but clearly unsettling. A large table dominated the center of the room, covered in archives, photographs, and a collection of haunting masks.

Evelyn's eyes widened as she approached the table. "This is it. This is where they have been conducting their operations."

Sarah began to go through the files, her face becoming more and more somber. "These documents detail more of The Circle's activities, including its current members and recent meetings. There is even a map that marks the locations where they have targeted the possible victims."

Holloway examined the photographs, recognizing several individuals of the public figures they had discovered. "These people are deeply involved. This information could blow up the case wide."

Evelyn's gaze fell on a corner of the room, where there was a large mirror adorned against the wall. The mirror was covered with strange symbols and carvings. She approached him cautiously, feeling an inexplicable attraction to him.

Touching the mirror, a hidden panel opened behind him, revealing a small safe embedded in the wall. Evelyn's hands trembled as she opened the safe and found a collection of disturbing objects: a diary, several old photographs, and a series of detailed plans for future activities.

The diary was full of cryptic entries, many of which referred to Evelyn and her family. It was clear that The Circle had been watching her closely. Evelyn's stomach churned as she read passages describing his plans to manipulate and control her.

Suddenly, a loud noise echoed through the warehouse, and the equipment froze. Footsteps and voices were approaching. They had been discovered.

Holloway beckoned them to hide, and they quickly placed themselves behind some boxes. The warehouse doors slammed open, and several masked figures entered, the presence of which sent shivers down Evelyn's spine. It was clear that The Circle was upon them.

Evelyn and her team held their breath as they listened to the intruders' conversation. They discussed a planned meeting with other senior members and discussed the need to address the growing pressure from the outside world.

As the figures scattered, Evelyn and her team emerged from their hiding places. They quickly gathered the documents and items they had found, knowing they needed to leave before they were caught.

Back at Evelyn's office, they reviewed the new evidence with a mixture of relief and anxiety. The diary and plans provided crucial information about The Circle's operations and its future intentions. They now had the means to expose the group and its elaborate network.

But Evelyn knew her fight was far from over. The Circle was more dangerous than ever, and they had to be prepared for whatever came next. The hidden chamber had revealed just how deep the conspiracy was, and Evelyn was determined to see it through to the end.

Chapter 20: The Final Confrontation

The atmosphere at Whispering Pines was charged with tension as Evelyn prepared for the final showdown. The hidden camera revelations had set a plan in motion, and Evelyn, Holloway, and Sarah were on high alert. The Circle was desperate, and their next moves would be crucial to bringing the sinister organization to justice.

Evelyn was standing at the edge of the woods, near Gabriel Stone's retreat, the place where she knew the final confrontation would unfold. The retreat, with its serene façade, concealed a dark underbelly of continual abuse and manipulation. She could feel the weight of the decision pressing heavily on her.

Holloway and Sarah joined her, their faces full of determination. "We've coordinated with the task force," Holloway said. "They are in position and ready to go as soon as we give the signal. But you have to be careful. The retreat is heavily guarded, and Stone will expect trouble."

Evelyn nodded. "I get it. We need to gather as much evidence as we can and make sure that the leaders of The Circle are stopped. This is our chance to end their reign of terror."

At dusk, the gardens of the retreat were bathed in a golden tone. Evelyn, Holloway, and Sarah made their way through the woods, avoiding patrols and security measures. They approached the entrance of the retreat, where the sound of joyful music and laughter betrayed the dark activities hidden within.

Inside the retreat, the atmosphere was deceptively calm. The guests mingled, oblivious to the sinister undercurrents of the place. Evelyn and her team slipped away from the guards, taking advantage of the night's coverage to navigate the hallways.

They arrived at the main chamber, where a meeting of the members of The Circle was taking place. Evelyn looked through a small window, watching Gabriel Stone in the center of the room. He was addressing the assembled members, his charisma evident even through the distorted lens of his hidden camera.

Stone's voice had a sinister tone as he spoke. "We are on the verge of a new era. Our influence is stronger than ever, and with the recent chaos, we will consolidate our power and ensure that our vision for this community endures."

Evelyn's heart raced as she prepared to move. "This is it. We have to get the evidence and get out before we get caught."

As they made their way to the evidence storage room, they came across several masked figures. Evelyn's pulse quickened, but Holloway's signal saw to it that they remained hidden. They managed to gain access to the storage room and began collecting incriminating documents and evidence.

As they worked, Evelyn's mind raced with the implications of their findings. The evidence not only implicated Stone, but also revealed connections to numerous high-profile figures. It was clear that The Circle's influence extended far beyond Whispering Pines.

Suddenly, the door of the warehouse burst open and several masked figures entered, their expressions filled with fury. Evelyn and her team were caught off guard and a struggle ensued. The confrontation was intense, with Evelyn, Holloway, and Sarah fighting to protect the evidence and themselves.

In the midst of the chaos, Evelyn saw Gabriel Stone approaching. He looked directly at her, with a cold smile on his lips. "Do you think you can stop us? You're too late. Our plans are already underway, and your little rebellion won't change anything."

Evelyn's eyes burned with determination. "We are not going to back down. This is over now."

As Stone and his enforcers drew closer, the sound of sirens pierced the night. The task force, led by Holloway's team, stormed the retreat, engaging in a fierce battle with members of The Circle. The chaos of the confrontation provided an opportunity for Evelyn and her team to escape.

They raced through the retreat, dodging the chaos and making sure they had the critical evidence. Outside, the task force worked to arrest the remaining members of The Circle. The sound of gunfire and screams filled the air as the battle reached its climax.

Evelyn and her team managed to get to safety, with the weight of the night's events pressing down heavily on them. The evidence they had gathered was crucial, and exposure of The Circle's operations was imminent.

As the sun began to rise, the retreat was assured, and the remaining members of the Circle were taken into custody. Evelyn, Holloway, and Sarah were together, watching the scene unfold. Dawn marked a new beginning for Whispering Pines and for Evelyn herself.

The battle had been won, but the scars of the past would remain. Evelyn knew that the journey ahead would be difficult, but she was determined to rebuild and find peace.

When Evelyn and her daughter Zoe visited the park later that day, the carousel spun gently in the breeze. Evelyn took a deep breath, feeling a sense of closure. The echoes of her past were finally being buried, and she was ready to embrace a new chapter in her life.

Chapter 21: The Unraveling Truth

The town of Whispering Pines was still reeling from the recent revelations, and the media frenzy had left no stone unturned. The arrest of Gabriel Stone and other high-ranking members of The Circle had shocked the community. As Evelyn and her team examined the fallout, they were faced with the daunting task of piecing together the full scope of the conspiracy.

Evelyn was in her office, surrounded by files and documents related to the activities of The Circle. The evidence they had recovered was overwhelming, and it was clear that the organization's reach extended far beyond what they had initially suspected.

Holloway entered the office with a grim expression. "We have made great progress. The forensic team has finished analyzing the documents and evidence of the withdrawal. There's a lot more to this than we thought."

Evelyn looked up, piquing her curiosity. "What did you find?"

Holloway handed him a folder. "The analysis revealed connections to several influential figures, including politicians, business leaders, and even some law enforcement officers. The Circle was not just a cult; It was a covert network that manipulated key actors to advance its agenda."

Evelyn's mind raced as she flipped through the documents. "Then, his influence reached the top. No wonder they were so entrenched."

Sarah joined them, carrying a stack of extra files. "We have also discovered more details about the people who were part of The Circle. Some of them were victims who were coerced into joining, while others were willing participants. It is a tangle of manipulation and control."

As they went through the files, Evelyn noticed a pattern emerging. Many of the names and connections were linked to cases of missing persons from the past, including the disappearance of his own mother. Realizing this, it hit him hard: The Circle had been orchestrating these events for decades, manipulating and controlling people for their own ends.

Evelyn's thoughts were interrupted by a phone call from Diane, her sister. Diane's voice was trembling but resolute. "Evelyn, I've been going through some old family records and I've found something that might be important. It's related to our mother's involvement with Gabriel Stone and The Circle."

Evelyn's heart raced. "What did you find?"

Diane explained that she had discovered a series of letters and documents hidden among her mother's belongings. The letters detailed meetings with Stone and referenced a plan to "clean up" certain individuals who were seen as threats to The Circle's goals. The documents also included sketches and notes on rituals that matched the descriptions Evelyn had discovered.

"This could be the missing piece" that we need, Evelyn said. "I'll come and check everything with you."

Evelyn arrived at Diane's house later that day, where her sister had left the papers on the dining room table. The letters and sketches were chilling, revealing the depth of her mother's involvement in The Circle's activities.

"This confirms what we suspected," Diane said. "Our mother was deeply entangled in this mess, and it's clear that she played a role in facilitating The Circle's operations."

Evelyn's mind reeled as she absorbed the information. "Now it makes sense. The images of the carousel, the rituals, everything was part of his method of control. Our mother's death was not an accident; It was orchestrated as part of his larger plan."

As they continued to go through the documents, Evelyn found one particular letter that stood out. It was a final communication from his mother, expressing regret and begging for forgiveness. The letter revealed that she had tried to distance herself from The Circle, but had not been able to escape its clutches.

Tears welled up in Evelyn's eyes as she read her mother's last words. "I was caught in a web of deception, like so many others. We have to make sure that their story is heard and that the truth is known."

Diane nodded. "We need to make sure that The Circle's legacy is exposed and that those responsible are held accountable."

With renewed determination, Evelyn and Diane began preparing a comprehensive report detailing their findings. They knew that disclosing the full extent of The Circle's operations would be crucial to preventing future abuses and ensuring justice for all victims.

As they worked late into the night, Evelyn felt a sense of closure begin to take shape. The truth was finally coming out, and the darkness that had plagued his life for so long was slowly receding.

Chapter 22: Shadows in the Past

The days after the revelations were a whirlwind for Evelyn and her team. Media coverage was relentless, and pressure to bring the remaining members of The Circle to justice was mounting. With Gabriel Stone and several key figures apprehended, Evelyn knew that the last pieces of the puzzle were crucial to closing this chapter of her life.

Evelyn and Holloway sat in his office, examining the remaining evidence. The task force has been making progress, but there are still unanswered questions. Evelyn's phone rang and she glanced at the caller ID before answering.

"Dr. Caldwell," said a voice on the other end. "I'm Detective Harris of the Whispering Pines Police Department. We have an advantage that could be significant. We have found something related to your mother's case."

Evelyn's heart skipped a beat. "What did you find?"

Harris explained that during a recent search of an abandoned property linked to The Circle, they had discovered a hidden room. Inside, they found old photographs, diaries and other items that seemed to connect directly to Evelyn's mother. The photographs included images of ritual gatherings and individuals who were previously unknown.

"We need them to come and review these items," Harris said. "Their experience could help us identify the significance of these findings."

Evelyn agreed to meet with Harris at the police department. Upon arrival, she was taken to a secure room where the items were displayed. The sight of her mother's belongings brought a flurry of excitement, but Evelyn focused on the task at hand.

Among the articles was a diary with entries detailing the inner workings of The Circle. The handwriting was unmistakably her mother's, and the entrances were filled with haunting accounts of the rituals and ceremonies she had been involved in. The diary also included names and dates that appeared to match some of the unsolved cases.

Evelyn carefully examined the photographs. One in particular stood out: a group of people gathered in a clearing, their faces obscured by animal masks. Among them was a woman who was eerily familiar. Evelyn gasped as she realized that the woman looked like someone she had seen before, but couldn't locate.

Harris noticed Evelyn's reaction. "Do you recognize anyone in these photos?"

Evelyn nodded, pointing to the woman in the photograph. "I think I've seen her before. It could be someone who's been involved with The Circle, or it could be a victim."

Harris took note of the information. "We will investigate this further. Their insights could be crucial in identifying these people and understanding their roles."

When Evelyn left the police department, she couldn't shake the feeling that they were about to uncover a critical piece of the puzzle. The diary and photographs provided a clearer picture of the scope of The Circle's activities, but many questions remained unanswered.

Back in her office, Evelyn went through the diary entries and photographs again. He noticed a recurring theme: references to a "final ceremony" that seemed to be a significant event for The Circle. The details were vague, but it was clear that this ceremony was central to their operations.

Evelyn decided to contact Diane for help. I needed to compare notes and see if Diane could provide any additional context based on her own research. Diane agreed to meet later that night.

When Diane arrived, they pored over the diary entries and photographs together. Diane's eyes widened as she recognized some of the names and references. "These entries match some of the details that our mother mentioned in her letters. The final ceremony must have been an important event for The Circle, possibly involving the highest-ranking members."

Evelyn's mind was running with possibilities. "If we can find out more about this ceremony, it might lead us to other key figures or places associated with The Circle."

As they continued their investigation, Evelyn received a call from Holloway. "We have managed to identify some of the individuals who appear in the photographs. It appears that they are connected to various organizations and have been using their influence to protect The Circle's activities."

Evelyn felt a surge of determination. "We need to expose these connections and make sure everyone involved is held accountable. The final ceremony could be the key to unraveling the rest of the conspiracy."

With this new clue, Evelyn, Diane, and Holloway worked tirelessly to put the final pieces of the puzzle together. They knew that the shadows of the past were approaching, but they were determined to shine a light on the truth and bring justice to those who had suffered.

As the investigation progressed, Evelyn felt a growing sense of determination. The journey had been arduous, but he was closer than ever to discovering the full extent of The Circle's dark influence.

Chapter 23: The Final Ceremony

Evelyn's sense of urgency had reached a fever pitch. The diary's cryptic references to a "final ceremony" seemed to be the key to understanding the full extent of The Circle's influence. With details gathered from various sources, Evelyn was convinced that uncovering the truth behind this event would be critical.

Research had revealed that the final ceremony was not just a ritual, but a high-profile event involving powerful figures. Details were scarce, but the importance of the ceremony in the operations of El Círculo was evident. The time had come for Evelyn to face this darkness head-on.

Evelyn, Diane, and Holloway gathered in his office, surrounded by documents, photographs, and notes. They had identified a pattern in the information they had gathered: the final ceremony seemed to occur on specific dates linked to astronomical events, hinting at ritual significance.

"This could be our window," Holloway said, pointing to a date in the coming weeks that will coincide with a lunar eclipse. "If the ceremony follows the pattern we've seen, it could take place during the eclipse."

Evelyn nodded, her mind racing. "We have to prepare for this. If El Círculo is still active and planning another ceremony, we have to be ready to intervene."

Diane, who had been researching possible locations for the ceremony, identified an isolated estate outside Whispering Pines that fit the diary's description. The estate was known for its elaborate gardens and hidden areas, making it a plausible location for the ceremony.

"We should keep an eye on the estate," Diane suggested. "If they're planning a ceremony, this is likely where it's going to take place."

As night fell, Evelyn, Diane, and Holloway approached the estate under cover of darkness. They parked their car at a safe distance and made their way through the dense woods surrounding the property. The estate stood ahead, with its tall iron gates and sprawling gardens lit by moonlight.

They found a viewpoint behind some bushes that provided a clear view of the entrance to the farm. The house seemed to be preparing for an event, with lights and decorations underway. Evelyn's heart pounded as she watched, knowing that the ceremony might be just around the corner.

After hours of waiting, the scene began to take shape. Figures began to arrive in elaborate costumes and masks, their identities obscured. The atmosphere was tense and Evelyn could feel the weight of the moment pressing on her.

As the guests gathered, Evelyn's thoughts turned to descriptions of the ceremony in the diary. The ritual involved intricate symbolism and elaborate rites, all designed to maintain control over the members of the Circle and reinforce their power.

Suddenly, the front door of the estate opened and a procession of masked individuals began to move towards a central area of the garden. Evelyn, Diane, and Holloway watched from their hiding place, taking note of the symbols and rituals being performed.

The ceremony was hauntingly reminiscent of the rituals described in the diary. The masked figures sang and performed complex movements, synchronizing their actions with the phases of the moon. Evelyn got goosebumps as she realized the full extent of the ritual's dark meaning.

Holloway signaled to the team to remain hidden as the ceremony reached its climax. The atmosphere was charged with ominous energy, and Evelyn could see that this was more than a symbolic event, it was a demonstration of The Circle's ongoing control and manipulation.

At the conclusion of the ceremony, the masked figures dispersed and the estate began to calm down. Evelyn, Diane, and Holloway took the opportunity to investigate further. They cautiously approached the estate, looking for any evidence that could be used to dismantle The Circle's operations once and for all.

Inside, they found a series of hidden rooms and chambers, filled with documents, photographs, and ritual artifacts. The evidence was overwhelming, but it was clear that The Circle's reach extended far beyond what they had previously imagined.

As they collected evidence and prepared to leave, Evelyn felt a mixture of relief and unease. The final ceremony had been a grim reminder of the darkness they faced, but it had also provided critical information about The Circle's operations.

With the evidence in hand, Evelyn knew the next steps were crucial. They had to expose the findings to the authorities and ensure that those involved were held accountable.

The confrontation with The Circle was coming to an end, but Evelyn understood that the battle for justice was far from over. The shadows of the past have brightened, but many challenges still lie ahead.

Chapter 24: Unraveling the Web

It was dawn when Evelyn, Diane, and Holloway left the estate, the weight of their discoveries on their shoulders. The evidence they had gathered was substantial, but Evelyn knew they had to act quickly to make sure they didn't go missing or be compromised.

Back at Evelyn's office, they spread out the documents, photographs, and artifacts they had recovered. Holloway's team had already been informed, and a plan was underway to raid the estate and arrest those involved in The Circle.

"The evidence we have is incriminating," Holloway said, examining a stack of documents. "But we have to make sure that we can link it all together and connect the dots with the people who are still out there."

Evelyn nodded, her eyes scanning a map of Whispering Pines and its surroundings. "We need to identify all possible connections between the members of The Circle and their activities. This is our chance to dismantle their network once and for all."

Diane, poring over a collection of photographs, suddenly pointed to a familiar face. "Look at this, this is one of the people who was present at the ceremony. I've seen it before in old newspaper clippings related to my research."

Evelyn bowed, recognizing the man as a prominent local figure. "We need to investigate their connections further. If involved, he could be a key player in The Circle's operations."

As they delved deeper into the connections, they discovered that several high-profile people had ties to The Circle. The network of influence extended to politics, business, and law enforcement. The realization was chilling: the Circle had become deeply embedded in the fabric of society.

Evelyn and Holloway decided to focus on the political and business leaders who seemed to have the most influence. They worked late into the night, compiling a list of names and cross-checking them against the evidence they had gathered.

When the sun rose, the work group mobilized for the raid on the farm. Holloway coordinated with other law enforcement agencies to ensure a coordinated effort. Evelyn felt a mixture of anticipation and anxiety, knowing that the raid would be a pivotal moment in her fight against The Circle.

At the farm, the agents entered with precision. The search uncovered a vast network of documents, financial records, and incriminating evidence linking The Circle to various illicit activities. Several arrests were made, including some of the key figures identified in Evelyn's investigation.

With the raid underway, Evelyn, Diane, and Holloway turned their attention to the remaining evidence. They needed to ensure that the full extent of The Circle's operations was exposed and that no stone was left unturned.

Evelyn's phone rang and she answered to hear Harris's voice. "Dr. Caldwell, we have identified some additional clues from the evidence collected. There are connections with offshore accounts and international organizations. This is bigger than we thought."

Evelyn's heart raced. "We need to follow up on these leads immediately. If the influence of The Circle extends beyond our borders, we have to act fast."

Harris agreed, and Evelyn, Diane, and Holloway began coordinating with international agencies to track down the additional leads. The scope of his research had expanded, and the stakes were higher than ever.

As the days passed, Evelyn's team worked tirelessly to piece together the final elements of her case. The evidence was overwhelming, and it became clear that The Circle's operations had been far-reaching and sophisticated.

In the midst of her efforts, Evelyn received a visit from Thomas and Zoe. His presence was a reminder of the personal toll the investigation had taken on his family. Evelyn felt a twinge of guilt, but she was determined to see the investigation through to the end.

"We are making progress," Evelyn reassured them. "But there is still work to be done. I need to carry this out."

Thomas nodded, his expression a mixture of concern and pride. "Just promise me that you will take care of yourself."

Evelyn nodded, knowing that her family's support was crucial as she faced the latest challenges ahead. The investigation was nearing completion, and Evelyn was committed to bringing justice to those who had suffered.

Upon returning to work, Evelyn felt a renewed sense of determination. The Circle's web was crumbling, and the truth was at hand. The fight for justice was about to end, but Evelyn knew that the road to resolution would be fraught with challenges.

Chapter 25: The Mask Uncovered

Morning light filtered through the blinds of Evelyn's office and cast long shadows over the room. Evelyn, Diane, and Holloway had been working nonstop to collect their findings and prepare for the next phase of their operation. With the raid on the estate revealing a treasure trove of evidence, they were now faced with the challenge of putting together the final puzzle.

Evelyn was engrossed in a series of documents detailing financial transactions when Diane burst in with a photograph in her hand. "You have to see this," Diane said, her voice tinged with urgency.

Evelyn took the photograph and examined it closely. It depicted a man wearing an ornate mask similar to those used in the ceremony. The background was unmistakably the interior of a luxurious office, adorned with symbols and artifacts reminiscent of The Circle's rituals.

"This was taken in the office of a high-profile business executive," Diane explained. "I recognize the decoration. It matches one of the places we identified during our research."

Evelyn's eyes narrowed as she realized the importance. "If this man is involved, he could link The Circle's operations to a major corporate entity. We need to act quickly before they can cover their tracks."

Holloway, who had been reviewing surveillance footage, looked up. "I've cross-referenced this with our database. The man in the photograph is Jonathan Blake, a prominent figure in the financial sector. His company has connections to several of The Circle's front organizations."

Evelyn felt a surge of determination. "We have to confront Blake and find out what he knows. If he is deeply involved, he might be able to provide crucial information about The Circle's network."

The team coordinated with law enforcement to arrange a meeting with Jonathan Blake. Evelyn felt a mixture of anticipation and apprehension as they approached her office in a skyscraper. Blake was known for his public persona of philanthropy and success, but Evelyn knew that beneath the surface was a connection to The Circle's sinister operations.

Inside Blake's opulent office, Evelyn, Diane, and Holloway were escorted to a private meeting room. Jonathan Blake entered, calm and collected, though a flash of nervousness flashed across his face as he recognized Evelyn.

"Dr. Caldwell," Blake greeted in a neutral tone. "What brings you to my office?"

Evelyn wasted no time. "We have evidence that links you to El Círculo. We need to know what you're involved in and what you can tell us about your operations."

Blake's expression remained cautious. "I have no idea what you're talking about. My company is dedicated to ethical business practices."

Diane placed the photograph on the table. "This was taken in his office. We know that you are connected to The Circle."

Blake's eyes widened slightly as he looked at the photograph. For a moment, he seemed to hesitate, then took a deep breath. "Okay, I'll tell you what I know. But you have to understand that this goes beyond me. The Circle is deeply rooted in various layers of society."

Blake revealed that he had been coerced into supporting The Circle's operations through financial contributions and manipulation. His company had been used as a front for money laundering and the facilitation of various illicit activities.

"They have files on everyone," Blake said, his voice trembling. "If you're trying to take them down, you have to be prepared for the consequences. They have people in key positions everywhere."

Evelyn and Holloway listened intently as Blake provided names and connections, revealing a network of people involved in The Circle's activities. The information was shocking and crucial, providing new leads for the investigation.

As she left Blake's office, Evelyn felt a sense of urgency. The pieces of the puzzle were fitting together, but the scale of The Circle's influence was greater than they had anticipated.

Back at their temporary headquarters, Evelyn, Diane, and Holloway reviewed the new information. They discovered additional links to powerful figures in both the business and political spheres. The extent of the Circle's infiltration was staggering, and the need to act quickly was paramount.

The team worked tirelessly to validate the new prospects and prepare for the next phase of their operation. Evelyn knew that exposing The Circle's network required meticulous planning and coordination with law enforcement agencies.

As night fell, Evelyn received a call from Holloway. "We have located a critical figure mentioned by Blake. We are preparing for an arrest and search warrant."

Evelyn's heart raced. "This could be the breakthrough we need. We are going to do it immediately."

The investigation was reaching a critical juncture. With the mask of deception beginning to lift, Evelyn felt a renewed sense of determination. The path to justice is clear, but the challenges ahead are significant.

Chapter 26: The Shattered Illusion

The rain fell incessantly on Millbrook, a heavy downpour that matched the severity of Evelyn's situation. His team had gathered all the crucial evidence they needed and was poised for a breakthrough. With Jonathan Blake's confession in hand, they were ready to take on another key figure in The Circle's elaborate network.

Evelyn, Diane, and Holloway were in their temporary operations center, a makeshift command post set up in a nondescript office building. The atmosphere was tense as they prepared for the next phase of their plan. Blake's information had pointed them to a high-profile political figure: Senator Richard Hayes, whose connections to The Circle were now evident.

"Senator Hayes has been a huge benefactor of a number of charities that The Circle has used as fronts," Holloway said, his voice grim. "Their involvement could provide the final pieces we need to dismantle their entire network."

Evelyn nodded. "We have to approach this carefully. Hayes has significant political influence and will likely have layers of protection. Our goal is to gather evidence without alerting you to our intentions."

The team coordinated with local law enforcement to obtain a search warrant for Hayes' property. As they prepared for the operation, Evelyn felt a mixture of apprehension and determination. The exposure of such a high-profile figure could lead to intense scrutiny and possible backlash.

In the dead of night, the team arrived at Hayes' opulent mansion. The estate was surrounded by high walls and security cameras, but Evelyn's team had carefully planned their approach to avoid detection.

The officers broke down the doors and began their search. Evelyn and Holloway were among the first to enter the mansion, navigating through a maze of luxurious rooms and hallways. The opulence of the Hayes home was both impressive and unsettling, a stark contrast to the darkness of The Circle's activities.

While combing the mansion, they discovered a room hidden behind a bookshelf in Hayes' private study. Inside, they found documents, photographs and personal effects linking Hayes to The Circle. The room was filled with evidence of illicit activities and interactions with other key members of the network.

Evelyn carefully examined the documents, her eyes widening as she realized the extent of Hayes' involvement. "This is it. We have found the evidence we need."

Holloway's team gathered the evidence and prepared for Hayes' arrest. The senator, who had been traveling, returned to his mansion to find law enforcement officers waiting for him.

When Hayes was taken into custody, he looked visibly shaken, his façade of carefully crafted respectability crumbling. Evelyn watched from a distance, feeling a sense of relief and unease. The arrest of a prominent political figure was a significant victory, but the aftermath is sure to be complicated.

Back at the operations center, Evelyn and her team began piecing together the final elements of their investigation. The evidence against El Círculo was piling up, but they needed to make sure that all connections were thoroughly documented and that arrests were secured.

Media coverage of Hayes' arrest created a media frenzy. The media reported on the high-profile case, and the public's reaction was a mixture of shock and outrage. The exposure of the Circle's infiltration of politics and business had far-reaching implications.

Evelyn met with Diane and Holloway to review her progress. "We have made significant progress, but we have to prepare for the consequences. The remaining members of the Circle are likely to try to cover their tracks or retaliate."

Diane, who had been closely following the news, added: "The media attention will put pressure on law enforcement to act quickly. We need to make sure that our evidence is strong and that we are prepared for any attempt to discredit our findings."

Evelyn agreed. "We have come too far to let anything jeopardize our progress. Let's stay focused and see this through to the end."

As the investigation moved into its final stages, Evelyn was acutely aware of what was at stake personally and professionally. The shattered illusion of the Circle's power was giving way to a new reality, one in which justice and truth were within reach. But the journey was far from over, and the challenges ahead would test his resolve.

Chapter 27: The Final Showdown

The first light of dawn barely pierced the heavy curtains of the operations center. Evelyn, Diane, and Holloway had been working tirelessly to prepare for the climactic confrontation with Gabriel Stone. With Senator Hayes in custody and The Circle's operations exposed, the team was now focused on overthrowing the cult leader and dismantling the remaining network.

Evelyn was sitting at a messy desk, examining the latest evidence. His thoughts were consumed by the impending confrontation. Gabriel Stone had been a shadowy figure throughout his investigation, and Evelyn knew that standing up to him would be the ultimate test.

"Everything is ready," Holloway said as he entered the room. "We have obtained a search warrant for Stone's welfare retreat and have coordinated with a task force. The operation will begin at 0600 hours."

Diane looked at Evelyn with concern. "Are you sure you're ready for this? The stone is dangerous and we don't know what to expect."

Evelyn took a deep breath, her determination unwavering. "We have come this far. We have to carry it out. Stone has been manipulating and abusing people for far too long. It's time to put an end to it."

As the sun began to rise, Evelyn and her team, accompanied by a tactical unit, headed to Gabriel Stone's wellness retreat. The retreat, situated on a sprawling estate outside of Whispering Pines, was a front for the cult's ongoing operations. The once serene environment now felt foreboding, its tranquility masking the sinister internal activities.

The team approached the retreat with caution. The estate was heavily guarded and security measures had been put in place to deter any unauthorized access. Evelyn's heart pounded as they prepared to break into the property.

"Remember, we need to find Stone and gather evidence of his involvement with The Circle," Holloway reminded the team. "Stay alert and follow protocol."

The agents made a precise entry into the property, quickly neutralizing the security personnel. Evelyn, Diane, and Holloway led the way through the labyrinthine corridors of the retreat, their footsteps echoing in the tense silence.

As they made their way into the estate, they came across several rooms filled with disturbing artifacts and documents related to the rituals of The Circle. The opulence of the surroundings contrasted sharply with the dark nature of the cult's activities. The further they went, the more oppressive the atmosphere became.

Finally they arrived at the central chamber, a large, ornate room with a high ceiling and elaborate decoration. The space was prepared for a ritual ceremony, with symbols and ceremonial objects. In the center of the room was Gabriel Stone, dressed in a ceremonial robe, his face partially obscured by a mask.

Stone's eyes narrowed at the sight of Evelyn and the team. "So, you have come to finish what you started. You're too late. The cycle continues and cannot be stopped."

Evelyn stepped forward, her voice firm. "It's over, Stone. We have the evidence and their operation is exposed. It's time for you to face justice."

Stone's expression twisted into a sneer. "Do you think you've won? The influence of the Circle is deeper than you can imagine. Even if you arrest me, others will take my place."

The confrontation escalated as Stone loyalists, dressed in ceremonial garb, emerged from the shadows. The team engaged in a tense standoff, with unwavering determination despite the growing danger.

In the midst of the chaos, Evelyn and Holloway maneuvered to secure the area and stop Stone. As they approached him, Stone attempted to flee, but his escape was thwarted by the tactical team. He was quickly restrained and taken into custody.

Evelyn took a moment to catch her breath, her heart racing with adrenaline. The retreat, once a symbol of The Circle's power, was now a scene of crumbling chaos. The evidence collected during the raid was substantial, providing a clear link between Stone and the cult's activities.

As the team completed their operation, Evelyn looked around the retreat, feeling a mixture of relief and determination. The exposure of The Circle's network and the arrest of Gabriel Stone were significant victories, but the impact on survivors and ongoing efforts to heal the wounds remained.

Holloway walked over to Evelyn, a satisfied expression on his face. "We have achieved it. The Circle is dismantled and Stone will face justice.

Evelyn nodded, her thoughts already shifting to the future. "We have made progress, but there is still work to be done. We have to support the survivors and make sure that The Circle's influence is eradicated."

Upon leaving the retreat, Evelyn felt a sense of accomplishment tempered by the reality of the long road ahead. The final showdown had brought down a formidable adversary, but the road to healing and rebuilding was just beginning.

Chapter 28: Aftermath and Reflection

The early morning sun cast a pale light on Millbrook, and its rays filtered through the dense fog that had settled over the town. Evelyn sat in her office, which had been cleared of its usual clutter, now a temporary haven of calm after the whirlwind of recent events. The arrest of Gabriel Stone and the dismantling of The Circle had brought a sense of closure, but the repercussions of his actions were far from over.

Evelyn's phone buzzed with messages and calls from various media outlets and colleagues eager for updates. She had to navigate the flood of inquiries while keeping her focus on the task at hand: making sure The Circle's network was completely dismantled and that survivors received the support they needed.

"Do you think this is over yet?" Diane asked, her voice tired but hopeful, as she walked into the office with a stack of files. "The Circle has been exposed, but the consequences will be significant."

Evelyn looked up from her desk, her expression thoughtful. "We have had a great impact, but the effects of their actions are profound. It will take time for everything to settle. Our priority now is to provide support to survivors and work to rebuild trust within the community."

Holloway arrived at the office with a folder full of documents. "We have gathered additional evidence of the withdrawal, and it is clear that Stone was the linchpin. But there's more work to be done. The media is covering the story extensively, and we have to handle the narrative carefully."

As they discussed their next steps, Evelyn's mind drifted to the survivors of The Circle's abuse. Many had come forward during the investigation, sharing their stories and seeking justice. The emotional toll of their experiences was evident, and Evelyn was determined to make sure they got the help they needed.

The team hosted a series of support sessions for survivors, partnering with mental health professionals and advocates. Evelyn and Diane were actively involved, offering advice and resources to those affected by The Circle's atrocities.

During one of the support sessions, Evelyn met with a group of survivors, with a mixture of relief and sadness on their faces. The stories they shared were heartbreaking, but there was a sense of solidarity between them. Evelyn listened intently, offering words of comfort and encouragement.

"This is just the beginning of your journey," Evelyn said, her voice soft but firm. "They have shown incredible strength in stepping forward, and now is the time to focus on healing and rebuilding their lives. We're here to support you every step of the way."

Survivors expressed their gratitude, and Evelyn felt a renewed sense of purpose. The road to recovery would be long and challenging, but she was committed to making a difference in their lives.

As the weeks passed, the media frenzy surrounding The Circle's downfall began to subside. The focus was on ongoing efforts to support survivors and address the wider issues of abuse and exploitation. Evelyn continued to work tirelessly, collaborating with advocacy groups and legislators to drive meaningful change.

One night, Evelyn found herself reflecting on the journey that had led her to this point. He was standing by the window of his office, watching the fog lift from the city. The turmoil and chaos of the past few months seemed to recede, replaced by cautious optimism for the future.

Diane joined her, remaining silent by her side. "It's been a tough road, but we've come a long way. How are you?

Evelyn turned to her sister, a tired but resolute smile on her face. "It's been a challenge, but I'm grateful for the support and the opportunity to make a difference. We have exposed the truth and helped bring about change. Now is the time to focus on healing and moving on."

As they watched the fog lift, Evelyn felt a sense of clarity and hope. The darkness that had enveloped his life and that of so many others was beginning to dissipate. The journey had been fraught with danger and heartach, but the light at the end of the tunnel was getting brighter and brighter.

Chapter 29: New Beginnings

The air was crisp and crisp, a welcome change from the oppressive atmosphere that had enveloped Millbrook for so long. Evelyn walked through the park with her daughter, Zoe, and the rhythmic rustling of leaves beneath her feet provided a soothing soundtrack. The park was a new favorite place for them, a place of respite and renewal.

Zoe, with her adolescent face now showing signs of resilience and healing, walked beside her, her silence saying it all. Recent events had deeply affected their relationship, but this departure was a step toward rebuilding their bond.

"Mom, I'm glad we're doing this," Zoe said quietly, looking at Evelyn. "It feels... different here."

Evelyn nodded, her gaze fixed on the carousel in the distance. It had been recently restored, its once faded colors are now vibrant and inviting. "It does, doesn't it? Sometimes, it's the little things that remind us how much has changed."

They approached the carousel, with its intricate horses and enchanting music that evoked a sense of nostalgia. Evelyn recalled the carousels of her childhood, the memories now tinged with pain and hope. He felt a mixture of emotions as he watched Zoe's anxious expression.

"Do you want to ride?" Evelyn asked, with a hint of a smile on her face.

Zoe's eyes lit up. "Yes, I would like to."

They climbed on the carousel, taking their places on two of the beautifully painted horses. As the journey began, the gentle spin and melodic melody created a sense of calm and normalcy that Evelyn had longed for.

As the carousel turned, Evelyn thought about the journey that had brought them there. The exposure of The Circle, the arrest of Gabriel Stone, and the ongoing efforts to support survivors had been monumental. However, the true measure of progress lies in everyday moments of healing and reconnection.

"Mom, are we really going to be okay?" Zoe asked, her voice filled with a mixture of hope and uncertainty.

Evelyn looked at her daughter, her heart aching with pride and love. "We are more than fine, Zoe. We start again. We have faced many things, but we are stronger because of it. Together, we will build a future full of hope and happiness."

The carousel continued its gentle turn, each rotation a reminder of the cyclical nature of life. For Evelyn, it symbolized the end of one chapter and the beginning of another: a new era of healing and renewal for her and her family.

As they disembarked from the attraction, Evelyn and Zoe walked hand in hand, their spirits buoyed by the simple joy of the moment. The park, with its lush greenery and vibrant carousel, offered a glimpse into the beauty that could be found even after the darkest of times.

Evelyn knew that the journey ahead would be full of challenges, but she was ready to face them with renewed strength. The cycle of abuse has been interrupted and now is the time to focus on creating a better future.

The sun began to set, casting a warm golden light over the park. Evelyn and Zoe sat on a nearby bench, watching the day turn to night. The quiet scene before them contrasted with the turmoil of the past, a symbol of the peace they were beginning to find.

"I'm proud of us," Evelyn said quietly, squeezing Zoe's hand. "We've come a long way and we have a lot to look forward to."

Zoe smiled, her eyes reflecting the fading sunlight. "Me too, mom. I think we're going to be fine."

As they sat together, Evelyn felt a sense of satisfaction and hope. The echoes of the past were slowly fading, replaced by the promise of new beginnings and the strength they had found in each other.

Chapter 30: The Final Echo

The serene morning light poured into the picturesque living room of Evelyn's house, casting long shadows that danced on the wooden floor. Evelyn sat by the window, her fingers gently running over the rim of her coffee cup. The house was quieter now, filled with an air of peaceful routine that had been a long time coming.

His phone buzzed on the table, a reminder of the constant stream of messages and calls that had become part of his daily life since the fall of The Circle. Evelyn had learned to handle the influx, focusing on important tasks while finding comfort in quiet moments.

Thomas entered the room, carrying a stack of newspapers. "Another day of media coverage," he said, placing them on the table. "It seems like they're still fascinated by the story."

Evelyn glanced at the headlines, noting the ongoing coverage of The Circle's exposure and the aftermath. The media frenzy had finally subsided, but the impact of the revelations continued to reverberate throughout the community.

"I suppose it's not surprising," Evelyn said, taking a sip of her coffee. "People need to process what happened, and the media is their way of doing that."

Thomas nodded, his gaze softening as he looked at Evelyn. "How are you?"

Evelyn smiled slightly, appreciating his concern. "I'm fine. The support we have received from friends, family, and the community has been overwhelming. It has helped us move forward."

As Evelyn and Thomas talked, Zoe walked into the room, her face beaming with excitement. "Guess what, Mom? I've been thinking about starting a support group for youth who have experienced trauma. I want to help others like us."

Evelyn's heart was filled with pride. "It's a wonderful idea, Zoe. You've always had such a compassionate heart. I'm sure you'll make a difference."

Zoe's eyes shone with determination. "I hope so. I want to create a space where people can share their experiences and find healing, just as we have been able to."

The family spent the day discussing Zoe's plans, exploring ways to support her initiative, and preparing for the future. Evelyn felt a deep sense of fulfillment as she watched her daughter channel her experiences into something positive.

Later that night, Evelyn took a leisurely stroll through the park where she and Zoe had ridden the carousel. The park was a symbol of his healing journey, a place where the echoes of the past had begun to fade.

As she walked, Evelyn reflected on the profound changes that had taken place. The cycle of abuse has been laid bare and justice has been served. The Circle had been dismantled and the survivors were finding their voices and paths to recovery.

At the edge of the park, Evelyn stopped to look at the carousel once more. There it was, a timeless symbol of joy and sadness, but now it represented a future in which hope could flourish. The music of the carousel, once an eerie reminder of the past, now played a melody of renewal and possibility.

Evelyn closed her eyes, letting the gentle breeze and the sound of carousel music wash over her. The last echoes of his tumultuous journey were drifting away, replaced by a new chapter full of promise and healing.

As she walked back home, Evelyn felt a renewed sense of peace. The past had left its mark, but it no longer defined her. He moved forward, embracing the future with hope and determination.